THE BATTLE OF BOXHILL

BY

LIAM McCANN

To Jessica,

Enjoy!

Liam

About the Author

This is Liam McCann's first children's novel. Liam was born in Guildford, England, in 1973. He attended Hurstpierpoint College and Staffordshire University, gaining a Bachelor of Arts degree in Sports Physiology and Psychology. Growing up, he excelled on the sports field, becoming county champion in three of the athletics field events and swimming to a national standard. He went on to win a British University medal in 1993. Instead of finding work in the sports industry, Liam formed a rock band that toured Europe for four years. The group's highlight came in 2001 when they played to five thousand people. Liam is currently working on his fifth action / thriller novel featuring hero Ed Sampson.

By Liam McCann

The Olympics Facts, Figures & Fun
Rugby Facts, Figures & Fun
Cricket Facts, Figures & Fun
The Sledger's Handbook
Born to Dribble
The Revised & Expanded Sledger's Handbook
The UFO Files
The 2012 European Football Championships

With Hans Potter

The Little English Boy

The Battle of Boxhill by Liam McCann

Published by Facts, Figures & Fun, an imprint of AAPPL Artists'
and Photographers' Press Ltd.
Church Farm House, Wisley, Surrey, GU23 6QL
info@aappl.com   www.aappl.com

Sales and distribution, UK and export
Turnaround Publisher Services Ltd.,
orders@turnaround-uk.com

This edition copyright©AAPPL 2012
Text copyright©Liam McCann 2011
First published 2012. Reprinted twice 2012

ISBN 9781904332145
Printed in UK by CPI Group (UK) Ltd, Croydon, CR0 4YY
Cover design by Martin Tidy www.martintidy.daportfolio.com/

THE BATTLE OF BOXHILL

I would like to thank Bulat Galimgereyev and Kevin Foo for giving me the idea for this book; Martin Tidy for his imaginative cover design; and publisher Cam Brown for his continued guidance and support and without whose input you would not be reading this book.

Liam McCann

1

It felt like any other spring day in Redlands Forest, but today was going to be different. The animals were unaware that they were being watched from a distance and that their lives were about to change forever.

A young male peregrine falcon swooped in low over the trees, testing his reactions by skilfully weaving through the smaller top branches. He then headed across an open field towards the chalk cliffs and his nest, stealing a quick, cautionary glance over his shoulder and feeling the wind rush through the glossy black and grey feathers on his neck. The sun was just poking its head above the eastern horizon, its long rays bringing welcome warmth after a chilly night.

The falcon rose sharply into the sunshine, spotted his nest away to his left and banked round to come in head on. When he was only a few yards from the nest he flared his wings, bringing his body upright and his feet forward. He used his wings as air brakes and touched down lightly on a flattish area high on the cliff face.

His mate stood to greet him, exposing two small red-brown eggs incubating under her warm belly. She rubbed her neck affectionately against his. "Are you ready for your big day, darling?"

He nodded slowly, nervously. "I've been practising on insects for the last hour but mid-air attacks are beyond me. My father is going to lose his patience."

She smiled, trying to restore confidence that was clearly draining away. "He'll never admit you're ready until you prove him wrong. I know you can do it. Show him!"

Ryker looked across the cliff face and shuddered. Two hundred yards to his right there was movement in his parents' nest. "Catching a mouse on the ground is no problem," he said, sighing. "They move so slowly. But taking another bird down in flight is a different matter."

She extended a wing and drew him close. "If you're going to provide all the food these two need, then today is the day. They're due at any moment."

He found himself drawing inspiration from her. She seemed much wiser and stronger than he at times. "I can't have my family going hungry," he replied, a sense of purpose filling him at last. "When I come back, it'll be with lunch." Deep down he realised that it was time to become an adult instead of relying on his parents for support, but today would provide his greatest test.

His thoughts were interrupted by the slow beat of strong wings. As always his startle reflex prepared him to fight or flee, but he realised it was only his father. He stepped back into the scrape to allow him to land and bowed his head.

Algar touched down with barely a sound. "Good morning," he said in a deep, cold voice. "How's my extended family?"

Safiyya smiled thinly. "One of us can't seem to relax, but the other three are fine."

Algar looked at his son and read the signs, the tension evident in his posture. "For heaven's sake, boy," he said quietly, "when are you going to grow up? It's really not that hard!"

"I don't think he shares your confidence," Safiyya said.

Algar huffed and turned away, his beak held high. "Well it's high time he earned his wings." He looked across the field and stretched. "Come on. Let's get this over with. You'll have to be self-sufficient by the time you leave the nest because there's not enough food around here to support all of us."

Ryker turned and gave Safiyya an anxious glance. "I guess I'll see you later."

She nodded, trying to encourage him, then gently drew a wing down his back. "Good hunting."

"We'll swing by the forest first," Algar said. "Follow me. And keep up!" He balanced on the cliff's edge and leaped off, spreading his wings to catch the early morning updraft.

Ryker followed his father, launching himself into space and allowing rising warm air to lift him above the sheer white walls. The sensation never failed to exhilarate him and was so liberating that his concerns melted away for a few brief moments. As they crossed the field, the light breeze fanned the long grass in wonderful patterns. He watched Algar thread his way through the trees and pluck a six-inch twig from the end of a branch with his sharp talons. Then he rose above the forest canopy. Ryker pulled up sharply and followed his father in a steep climb. Soon he could see for miles in every direction, with the cliffs an indistinct white blur in the distance.

Algar soared on the currents to conserve energy. "Okay, son, it's time," he said. "You know the drill. I'm going to drop the stick. You must catch it before it hits the ground. Let's try and get it right today, huh?"

Ryker knew his father would give the stick a head-start. He tried to calm his nerves by imagining a successful strike, but he could only picture himself missing it and hurtling into the ground at full speed. "Okay, I'm ready," he mumbled eventually.

Algar released the stick and watched it tumble end over end. After what seemed like an eternity to Ryker, he gave his son the nod. "Well? What are you waiting for?"

Ryker folded his left wing under his body and rolled onto his side, then put his head down and straightened his shoulders. He flapped his wings and accelerated hard until gravity was giving him all the help he needed. He drew his wings into his body to present the most streamlined shape possible and was soon falling so fast he almost lost control of his stomach.

The air rushed past at an alarming rate. Breathing was a waste of time so he concentrated on keeping the stick in sight instead. Try as he might, however, he couldn't seem to tuck his wings in close enough. He knew he wasn't going to make it but he wanted to impress his father so held the dive as long as he could.

Despite making ground on the twig, the race was lost. It hit the ground and bounced a couple of times in the long grass. Ryker was still careering towards the field. He tried to spread his wings and pull out of the dive but the wind pressed them into his flanks. The air tore at his feathers and flipped him over. He opened his mouth in terror as the ground rushed up to meet him and in that instant he knew he was going to die. His life might have flashed before his eyes had there been time but he closed them tight, held his breath and waited for the bone-crushing impact.

Instead there was a blow from behind. He was gripped tightly at the neck and tail by a pair of powerful, destructive talons. Out of the frying pan and into the fire! Instant death from hitting the ground had been replaced by who knew what sort of death at the hands of a monstrous predator. He was relieved to find, however, that this new terror turned out to be none other than his father. Ryker's relief was short-lived.

"You idiot!" Algar barked, dropping him unceremoniously in the grass. "That was reckless, incompetent and plain stupid!"

"Sorry, Dad," Ryker said sheepishly. "I didn't want to give up in front of you."

"It's time you learned from your mistakes," Algar said bluntly as he tried to teach Ryker to become independent. "Anyone watching you would have thought you mad.

Make sure you get it right next time."

"I can't do it," Ryker replied sullenly.

Algar couldn't hide his impatience. "Follow me. Keep in my slipstream and take over when I peel away. And you'd better not mess up again because I won't be there to save you."

Ryker waited while his father collected the stick and followed him back into the air. Once they'd reached the right height, he took a few deep breaths to try to steady his nerves. Eventually he gave his father a nod. "Okay, I'm ready."

Algar released the stick once more and counted to five. Then he swept past Ryker and rolled over. Ryker followed immediately, knowing that his father's better technique would take him away unless he could keep on his tail. The wind began to rush past his face. No more than a few seconds passed before his father tucked his wings back and accelerated hard. Ryker continued with the eye-watering dive, making tiny adjustments to the leading edges of his wings to stay in control.

His peripheral vision blurred so that the only things he could see were his father and the sliver of wood tumbling far below them. As they hurtled towards the ground, Algar suddenly pulled away to let his son go for the kill. Ryker steadied himself and took a moment to judge his height. He'd have to strike in the next few seconds. He flicked his right wing to bring him directly behind the twig, then extended his talons and struck hard. Success! He flared both wings to control the dive and levelled out, looking to his father for approval. But in his moment of glory he got complacent and fumbled the stick. His father swept past and settled in the field.

Ryker joined him, his face a picture of disappointment. "Sorry. That wasn't too clever."

"A recurring theme, don't you think?" Algar snapped.

"I am trying, you know."

Algar fixed his son with a hard stare. "It didn't take me this long to learn."

Ryker couldn't help himself. "Perhaps your father was a better teacher."

Algar's eyes narrowed. "Learn some respect, boy. Don't bite the talons that feed you."

Ryker knew he'd overstepped the mark and wisely backed down. His father's temper was legendary. "Can we give it another go?"

"No," Algar replied. "We'll head back to the nest to talk things through. We're not accomplishing anything here."

About half a mile away a raven and a magpie perched on the end of a thick branch overhanging the far corner of the field. Below them a robust metal fence stood fully eight feet tall. Barbed wire circled the top two feet and a low hum from a box mounted halfway up the post told them the fence was electrified. Signs every hundred feet or so warned trespassers to keep out or face prosecution. The fence divided the farmer's field and the picturesque Redlands Forest opposite from Ravenswood, the gamekeeper's vast, sprawling estate that took up most of Boxhill. Part of the old wooden fence still remained but it hadn't been maintained since the gamekeeper had moved in.

A pigeon landed in a dilapidated hide a short distance away and searched for insects in the rotting wood. She came across several woodlice and started feeding.

The raven kept one eye on the falcons and another on the nests on the cliff to their right. "The chicks must be about to hatch," he said, turning to the magpie. "We should strike while the father and son are away from nests. We'll be breaking our territorial agreement but that time has come."

The pigeon stopped feeding and cocked an ear in their direction.

The magpie's one beady eye took in every detail. Her other eye socket was dark and empty and hinted at her violent past. "With only the two females protecting the eggs, we'll overrun the nests in minutes. I'll gather the asylum of cuckoos for the attack. How many can you muster from your conspiracy?"

Dillon shrugged. "A dozen or so."

Jolenta nodded, pleased. "I'll lead the raiding party on the nest itself while you fly cover. Even if we lose a couple of cuckoos, we can still escape with the eggs and get back here before the falcons know what's hit them."

The pigeon shook her head slowly and inched closer to the two birds on the branch above. Her heart was pounding in her chest. She had to warn the birds living in Redlands that the ravens were about to attack, but she couldn't tear herself away until she'd heard more. She hopped even closer and hoped they wouldn't notice her on the ground below.

The jet black raven pointed his pitted beak towards the nests. "We need to sacrifice a cuckoo anyway. As soon as the young male falcon is ready, his father will want him to attack live prey."

Jolenta understood immediately, an evil look crossing her face as her black and white feathers ruffled in the light breeze. "We're going to need a diversion to lure them away. I know just the bird but I'd better not give her the full story in case she develops an aversion to flying suicide missions." She glanced back up at the nests and noted their exact positions. "We go in half an hour, Dillon."

The raven didn't like taking orders from a female but for now he had no choice. He leaped off the branch and disappeared into the trees.

Jolenta flew south along the fence before cutting into a clearing. The cuckoos were waiting for her but they were clearly nervous. She singled one out and took him aside. "How many spies do we have in the Redlands Forest, Flint?" she asked.

Flint wouldn't look her in the eye because he knew it irritated her, so he stared at his feet instead. "Only one has survived. I slipped him in with a pigeon family last week. They're so stupid they'll never notice, but the chick isn't old enough to report back yet."

"Let me know as soon as you hear anything," she said firmly.

The sickly grey cuckoo nodded, the black stripes on his chest compressing and looking like the bars of a prison cell. "A couple more days and he'll give us all we need."

"Gather your flock for the attack," she continued. "But send me Kinsey first. I have a special mission for her."

"My sister?"

Jolenta fixed him with her one malevolent black eye. "Do it now."

Ryker turned at the flutter of smaller wings and looked over his father's shoulder. A pigeon was approaching the nest. This was extremely unwise given his father's mood so she must have something urgent on her mind. She tried to land on the ledge but Algar turned and shooed her away.

"You've got a nerve coming up here," he said. "If I wasn't busy teaching my son I'd make a meal of you. Now, be off!"

The pigeon circled and flew in closer. "I think Dillon is planning something," she gasped. "I thought I'd better warn you."

Algar waved his wings angrily. "We've nothing to fear from him or his flock. He respects our truce."

Safiyya's ears pricked up. "Perhaps we should hear her out, Algar. I don't trust that raven."

Algar took a deep breath and fixed her with an icy stare. "Please, Safiyya, you're alarming Ryker! We falcons don't take advice from anyone, let alone a brainless pigeon." He turned back to his son. "It's time to continue your training." He then leaped off the cliff and scared the pigeon out of his way.

Ryker followed, casting a forlorn glance over his shoulder and noting Safi's uneasy look.

2

The two falcons climbed swiftly into the sky on thermal currents that were even stronger than they had been that morning. There wasn't a cloud to be seen.

Ryker drew alongside his father. "What was that about?"

Algar shook his head. "Never you mind. Just don't fly over the Ravenswood estate. I can't have you mixing with the birds there. They are beneath us in the pecking order but they outnumber us so we observe an uneasy truce: they won't fly over Redlands and we won't encroach on Ravenswood. It's not a perfect arrangement but it keeps the peace."

"I've never liked those woods," Ryker replied. "They give me the creeps."

"Promise me one thing," his father continued seriously, "if you ever find yourself over there, don't land in the far corner of the estate."

Ryker frowned. "Why not?"

"Every time I've come back to these cliffs I've heard rumours of a wild animal living up there," Algar explained. "Apparently it feeds on sheep and has even attacked cows."

"If you're trying to scare me, it's working," Ryker said, shuddering at the thought of bumping into an animal that could take on a cow. He thought his father might be spinning a tall tale to try to warn him off the gamekeeper's farm, but there was a concerned look in his eyes. "I've no intention of flying over there anyway."

"Good," Algar said. He was about to guide his son

through another mock attack when he spotted a movement far below. He smiled to himself. Here was an opportunity to raise the stakes. "There's a cuckoo. It's time for your first mid-air kill."

"I'm not ready," Ryker replied nervously. "Can't we continue with the stick?"

"No," Algar said, huffing in exasperation. "All those blasted cuckoos do is take over other birds' nests. Remember what happened when you were younger? This is your chance to redeem yourself, partially at least."

Ryker's face fell. He still felt guilty for not being able to protect his sister when they were younger. He took a deep breath and tried to use her memory to guide him. He could feel the tightness in his wings from all the exertion, but the anticipation in his stomach soon overruled it. His heart beat powerfully and his talons clenched. There was no question now that he would do it.

"Can I follow you?" he asked tentatively.

Algar shook his head. "If you're serious about raising a family in a new territory, you must do this on your own. Use the sun to shield your approach."

Ryker nodded and took another deep breath to try to steady his nerves. He glanced down and saw the cuckoo meandering aimlessly below. He tried to predict where the bird would be when he struck and rolled over to begin his attack. Having honed his skills that morning, he felt a little more confident. The cuckoo had no idea he was bearing down on it like a lightning bolt. Ryker brought his wings into his body and arrowed in with deadly accuracy, the wind ruffling his dark neck feathers once more.

He made a slight adjustment when he was about fifty yards behind the prey bird and then flared his wings for the strike, his talons arcing forward menacingly. But at the last moment the cuckoo sensed he was there. It glanced over its shoulder, a look of terror crossing its face. It veered off sharply but the change of direction merely brought about a mid-air collision, which threw Ryker into a spiral. He felt a surge of adrenalin as he righted himself and gave chase.

The cuckoo darted towards the estate as if the dark woods would protect it. Ryker struggled to keep up. In level flight his advantage all but disappeared. He angled in for another strike and was only a few yards behind when the cuckoo crossed the electric fence. Ryker thought about following it into the woods but remembered what his father had said and pulled up in time.

In all the excitement he hadn't noticed what was going on around him however. He suddenly realised that his father was still circling high above, his attention fixed on the distant cliffs. Sensing danger, Ryker climbed sharply to join him. Algar was heading back to the cliffs at full speed and he had to strain every sinew to keep up.

"What's wrong, Dad?" Ryker shouted above the wind.

His father slowed and allowed him alongside. "I thought I heard your mother's distress call from the nest."

Ryker couldn't quite read the urgency in his father's voice. His hearing wasn't as acute and he'd been in the middle of a stooping dive when the call had come. As they drew closer, the situation became clearer and his forehead creased with worry. There were birds jostling for position around the nests and he could clearly hear the distress calls.

Algar suddenly realised there was a full scale attack underway. "It's those blasted cuckoos!" he shouted as they approached. "They're breaking our agreement. This is no place for you. Stay out of the way but look out for the ravens because they usually work together."

Ryker didn't have time to feel fear. He was thrown into a pitched battle and his natural instinct for self-preservation took over. He pulled up and searched the sky above the cliffs. His father had been right: there were at least ten ravens circling the nest. He looked back and was pleased

18

to see a cuckoo already tumbling out of the air.

Leaving his father to protect the nests, Ryker climbed sharply, but the flock of ravens suddenly descended on him! If Algar had seen how many ravens there were, he would never have left Ryker alone against them, for although he was bigger and stronger than any individual, he was outnumbered by the aggressive birds and was a complete novice at air-to-air combat.

A large black shape whipped in front of him, then another and another. Ryker swung round as the ravens raced in before peeling off at the last minute, their wings flapping noisily in his face. They were trying to confuse him. One strayed even closer and lashed out with its talons. The blow caught Ryker in the chest and nicked twin furrows in his flesh. He gasped as a thin trickle of blood stained his feathers. This was turning nasty.

Dillon saw that he was struggling and scythed straight into him, knocking him onto his back. The raven then swung his heel hard at Ryker's head, sending him tumbling out of the sky. Dillon left him to his fate amongst his ravenous flock and soared above the cliff to check on the cuckoos.

Ryker shook his head and came to his senses just in time. He then decided to go on the offensive. He flared his wings and flipped round to chase one of the ravens. He was determined to show them just how powerful he was and struck with terrifying force, his talons cutting into the raven's back. The animal screeched in pain and tried to fight back, but it was no use. The falcon was too strong. Ryker squeezed his talons and dropped the dying raven.

He watched it spiral to the ground before facing the other birds. They were gathering for a strike. He knew it was time to beat a hasty retreat so turned and ran for the cliffs. The ravens were hot on his tail but he didn't look back and was soon circling the nests.

He couldn't see his father at first but he soon spotted him battling with three or four cuckoos. His mother,

Mercia, was also struggling to fend off an attack. Ryker rolled sideways to help but the move left his flank exposed. Before he could protect himself, three ravens overwhelmed him, hissing and squawking to scramble his senses. He fought the first one off with a vicious swipe from his right leg, but the second caught him by the wing and twisted hard. Ryker screeched as the joint dislocated and he began to fall. The third raven struck hard at his head and he briefly lost consciousness.

When he came to he was falling in a long slow spiral, his right wing useless. He flapped feebly with his left but it only made the spin worse and the ground rushed up to meet him. His father shouted something before becoming lost amidst the cuckoos. Ryker tried to call back but no sound came. He watched in slow motion as the ravens regrouped and attacked the nests. Somewhere in the distance he heard Safiyya crying out. He tried once more to return her call but his head hit the cliff and he tumbled to the ground.

3

A man approached a stile at the southern end of the thirty-acre field. He climbed over it into the foot-long grass. His two dogs knew this was the best part of the walk and they strained against their leads. The farmer unleashed them but told them both to sit down before giving them the go-ahead to run free. They then charged into the field, jumping and cavorting as if it was the first time they'd ever been outside.

As Gordon followed on behind, he noticed a pile of feathers lying in the grass to his right. He knelt beside the dead bird and shook his head. It was a cuckoo. And it had clearly been attacked. The farmer knew the carcass would be devoured by the earth in a couple of days so he continued tracking the dogs. It wasn't long before he noticed another dead bird. This was a large raven, and it bore similar scratch marks to the cuckoo. It was not uncommon to find the odd dead bird on his walks but the closer Gordon got to the cliffs the more there seemed to be.

He climbed the stile over the top fence and waited for the dogs. He then put them back on their leads and walked the footpath at the base of the cliff. Here the signs of battle were more obvious. There were blood-stained cuckoo feathers beside the path and, every thirty paces or so, dead ravens. As he passed an elm tree underneath the steepest part of the cliff, he noticed yet another bird. The dogs ran up to it expectantly and Gordon had to pull them back sharply. This was a young peregrine falcon.

Gordon played the scene back in his mind. Cuckoos

were notorious for attacking other birds' nests while the ravens flew cover. It was a shame they'd attacked the falcons because they were so rare. Their cliff-top nests usually gave them protection from the parasitic cuckoos, but not this time. He shielded his eyes and scanned the cliff. He could just make out the two falcon nests, but there was no movement in either. He was too late; the battle had been fought and won.

He knelt beside the dead falcon but got quite a surprise when one of its eyes flickered open. The dogs jumped backwards so Gordon tied them to the fence. He couldn't have them alarming the falcon while he tended to it. There was fear in its eyes and it was clearly distressed. Gordon was no vet but he noticed the odd angle of its wing and guessed it was broken. There were also two bloody gouges on its chest and a number of scrapes around its head.

He couldn't leave the peregrine because he knew a fox would take it come nightfall, or the crows and magpies would wait for it to die before dropping in for an easy meal. Gordon always wore a wide-brimmed hat on his walks so he gently lifted the bird and placed him inside. The falcon tried to resist and half-heartedly pecked at his hands but the fight soon went out of him. Gordon undid his scarf and wrapped it round the bird to keep it warm. Then he collected the dogs and headed back across the field to his farm, the early afternoon sun bathing them in a warm glow.

The dogs curled up in their baskets on the rear porch and Gordon took the falcon inside his old English character farmhouse. He placed the hat on the kitchen table next to a woman's photo. He stared at the picture for a while and a tear rolled down his cheek. He inhaled deeply, took the photo into the living room and slid it into a drawer in his Welsh dresser with all the others. He slowly removed his wedding ring and placed it on top. Then he sighed, bowed and eased the drawer closed before disappearing into the study to make a quick phone call.

Having hung up, he collected his car keys from a hanger by the front door and pulled on his trusty Barbour jacket. He didn't bother locking up or letting the dogs in because he wouldn't be long. He placed his hat on his Range Rover's passenger seat and started up the road to the local animal sanctuary, hoping that Simone would be able to save the young falcon.

He pulled up in front of the building ten minutes later and parked between two large trucks. Simone had come out to meet him. They were old friends and embraced warmly.

"Don't mind the film crew," she said. "They're just packing up for the day."

Gordon wondered what all the vans were doing in the car park, but he knew that Wildlife SOS, the sanctuary's charity, often filmed promotional videos in the area. "Aren't they supposed to be covering this year's festival?"

Simone nodded. "They're doing a special feature on the cycle race and the vineyard on Boxhill. Let's hope the weather's better than last year. The vines were almost killed by the late frost and the grape yield was down."

"Don't I know it," Gordon said, patting his generous stomach. "My stock of rosé ran out months ago."

"You should cut down," she replied, winking. "You know there's talk of changing the town's coat of arms at the festival's AGM."

"To what?" Gordon asked. "They've had the cockerel on it for hundreds of years."

"I think they wanted a shield that reflected the county's more interesting wildlife," Simone replied. "There was a rumour going round that the Surrey Puma might get a look in."

Gordon laughed loudly. "We both know that story is a complete myth. If you really believe that a couple of big cats escaped from an eccentric owner twenty years ago, you've been consuming too much of the local produce."

Simone smiled, revealing a set of perfect white teeth, but didn't reply. She didn't want to worry him by telling him that there had been a spate of attacks on livestock in the last few weeks. So she changed the subject and pointed to the hat. "Look at this poor chap."

Gordon handed her the falcon. "I found him on the footpath beneath the cliffs. I hope I'm not too late."

Simone carefully peeled back the scarf, adjusted her reading glasses for a closer look and whistled. "Isn't he beautiful? And rare too. We don't see many falcons around here any more. Their nests are terrorised by the cuckoos, and poachers keep trying to steal their eggs. They're extremely valuable, you know."

Gordon nodded, things becoming clearer. "There's something of an illegal trade in peregrines. Can you help this one?"

Simone ushered him into a small medical room just inside the sanctuary's main entrance and pushed the door closed behind them. "Let's hope so."

He noticed a number of animal paintings on the walls. "Who's the artist?" he asked. "Some of these pieces are exquisite, especially the one of the eagle taking a fish from the river in the Highlands."

Simone's hazel eyes lit up. "Actually, they're mine."

Gordon studied each painting closely. "I'm no expert but I think you should try your hand at the next coat of arms if the town is serious about changing it."

She bowed her head modestly, her cheeks flushing. "You're a true friend, Gordon, but I don't think they're good enough." She then lifted the falcon out of the hat, removed the scarf and placed him on a table in the centre of the room. After a couple of minutes she stood back and sighed. "He's going to need some TLC because his right wing is dislocated. I should be able to put it back but it's going to hurt and he'll need to stay here for a day or two."

"What about the scratches?" Gordon asked.

Simone spread the falcon's feathers and checked the wounds. "They're superficial," she said at last. "The two on his chest are only skin deep and will heal naturally. I'll give him some cream to ease the pain. The bump on his head is a bit more serious but it's not life-threatening. With luck, he'll be up and about in forty-eight hours or so."

Gordon sounded surprised. "That soon?"

Simone had noticed the determined look in the bird's eyes. This one was a fighter. She stroked his neck affectionately. "I'll call as soon as he's ready. I think it's only right that you should release him."

"Thank you," Gordon said. "I'd like that."

The sanctuary owner held the door open and they walked across the car park. Gordon climbed into the Range Rover and wound the window down. They kissed on the cheeks and he eased out onto the main road. Simone waited until the car had disappeared before heading back to the medical centre. She'd always had a soft spot for the farmer but could tell he was still grieving.

She looked down at the falcon and smiled thinly, as if apologising for the pain she was about to inflict. She massaged his wing until she felt it was ready to pop back into place. The bird opened and closed its beak as if trying to communicate with her, then closed his eyes and tensed. Simone gripped him firmly around the middle and eased the joint back into its socket. The falcon twitched uncomfortably but made no sound. Simone rubbed his back and spoke soothingly until he settled down. Then she opened one of the cupboards and removed a small jar of ointment. She parted the falcon's breast feathers and treated his cuts. When she was happy, she turned her attention to the bumps on his head.

By the time she finished she was confident he'd make

a good recovery. She hated to put the animals in cages but there was no other option. She gently carried the falcon into a room filled with injured animals and placed him in a cage next to a kestrel. Then she dimmed the lights and slipped out to deal with the next casualty.

Despite the dull, throbbing ache in his wing, Ryker felt much better. But he couldn't help feeling guilty for not being able to protect his family. Unpleasant memories from his childhood came flooding back and he prayed that Safiyya and the chicks had survived.

He had a difficult relationship with his father but there was no doubt in his mind that Algar would put his life on the line for them. Surely his father was powerful enough to have seen off the attack. Ryker had to return to the nest as soon as possible to find out.

A voice from the next cage made him jump. "This is where you tell me that I should see the other guy."

Ryker struggled to his feet but was still a little wobbly. "I think they came off better," he mumbled.

The kestrel nodded slowly. "So there was more than one, eh?"

"A flock of ravens attacked us while cuckoos tried to take our nests," Ryker replied.

The kestrel in the next cage seemed to understand. "Nasty pieces of work those ravens. Thankfully they don't stray too close to my territory."

"Where's that?" Ryker asked.

"I keep birds out of the way of aircraft coming into the airport," the kestrel replied. "We can't afford too many bird strikes or the safety board grounds the planes."

"So you scare them off," Ryker said, looking impressed. "How did you end up in here?"

The kestrel bowed sheepishly. "I was chasing a couple of blackbirds away when I got taken out by a light aircraft.

It knocked me clean into next week. I don't remember anything after that until I woke up here. I thought I was dead for a while."

"Sounds like you were lucky to survive," Ryker said.

"Tell me about it," the kestrel replied. "If I'd been a couple of feet to the left I'd have gone through the propeller instead of hitting the wing. Diced kestrel, anyone?"

Ryker smiled at the older bird's turn of phrase. It was only then that he noticed the kestrel was missing a leg. "Did you lose it in the accident?"

"Took it clean off. Can't complain though. I'm still here."

"I'd be hopping mad," Ryker said, before he realised how awful the joke was.

The kestrel rolled his eyes, collapsed onto his back, twitched and then played dead. "That's the worst line I've ever heard," he muttered between groans. "But at least you're trying to make me feel better."

"How much longer do you think you'll be here?" Ryker asked.

The other bird shrugged and rolled onto his good leg. "Do you know what? I haven't got a clue. I hope it's not long because I've got a family to feed." He could tell from Ryker's reaction that this was a tender subject, so he broached it carefully. "Do you want to talk about it?"

Ryker wasn't sure he wanted to discuss what had happened but eventually decided to tell the kestrel. Maybe he'd know what to do. When he finished he waited for the other bird to speak.

"Sounds like they were after your eggs," the kestrel said slowly. "They fetch a good price on the black market. You peregrines are worth a pretty penny, believe me."

"Will you help me find them when we get out of here?" Ryker asked.

"Not sure I'm up for another scrap just yet," the kestrel replied. "And my family will be beside themselves with worry."

Ryker saw the kindness in the other bird's face and understood his desire to get home. "How do you know which humans to trust?" he asked. "My dad is always warning me to steer clear of them."

"That," Hawkins said slowly, "isn't as easy as it sounds. This is my first trip to the vet and she seems caring and trustworthy, as do my employers at the airport, but if there are poachers after your eggs, then it's a different matter. Always go with your instincts. And if they're carrying a gun, wing it."

"I'll bear that in mind," Ryker said uneasily, suddenly remembering that he didn't know the kestrel's name. "By the way, what do they call you?"

The kestrel smiled and stretched his wings. "Hawkins, but you can call me," he paused for a moment as if about to announce something of earth shattering importance, "Hawkins."

Ryker laughed, his worries taking a momentary backseat. "I'm Ryker. It's nice to meet you."

4

The gamekeeper checked the perimeter fence. The pheasant he'd winged had bolted and was probably hiding in the undergrowth. He swore loudly, tugged on his Rottweiler's lead and headed for his farm in the middle of Ravenswood, determined to empty the shotgun at the next animal he came across.

He didn't have to wait long. A solitary blackbird flitted through the trees above him. Nigel shouldered the gun, aimed at the defenceless bird and pulled he trigger. The report was deafening, the trees bordering the path magnifying it tremendously. The blackbird fell. Several birds broke for the late afternoon sun, which was just dropping below the horizon, its rays casting lengthening shadows through the woods.

Nigel pulled the dog back and marched over to the crippled bird. Killing it was an act of mindless cruelty, no more. He grunted, dropped the bird's remains in a small plastic bag and continued down the path as if nothing had happened.

He'd only taken another twenty paces when the dog suddenly stopped and growled. The gamekeeper tugged sharply on his lead but he raised his hackles and bared his teeth and refused to budge. "Come on, Rory," he said sternly, whipping the dog's rear end. "This is no time for playing games."

Rory yelped but still refused to move. Nigel checked the clearing to see what was bothering him and noticed a large woolly mass wedged between a couple of tree branches about ten feet off the ground. The gamekeeper tried once more to pull Rory along but the dog was having none of it so he dropped the lead and approached alone.

There were deep gouges in the sheep's remains and a steady stream of blood stained the base of the tree. The animal had obviously not been here long. Nigel shuddered as he inspected the carcass. It looked like it had been ripped apart by a powerful animal before being dragged into the tree to be consumed later. He cast his mind back a couple of years to when he'd lost sheep in similar circumstances, but none were this close to the house. That spate of killings had soon stopped and the case remained unsolved, but the mysterious killer seemed to have returned.

It was then that he got the impression he was being watched. He whirled round but there was nothing there. The dog was whimpering with fear now. A rustling in the bushes to his left spooked him and he almost froze. Quivering with terror he ran for the farm, his Rottweiler charging after him as if trying to escape Cerberus, the three-headed dog that guarded Hades in ancient mythology. The rustling seemed to follow them for a bit and then stop. Nigel glanced over his shoulder, nausea rising in his stomach. He fell into the gate leading to the yard, his breath coming in great pants, heart pounding like a jack-hammer. He staggered inside and slammed the gate behind the dog. He peered back into the woods but couldn't see anything. There was only the gentle whisper of leaves in the breeze. He took a deep breath to steady his nerves and crossed the muddy yard, determined to carry a gun at all times.

As he approached the outbuildings the excited chatter from inside died down. The animals could tell when Rory and the gamekeeper were around and knew it was a good time to keep quiet.

A single raven was perched on a heavy steel fencepost as if awaiting his master's return. Nigel barely acknowledged Dillon. He slid the bolts back on an old stable door, flicked

30

on the lights and stepped inside. The dog waited at the door.

The stable reeked of manure, and piles of rotting hay only added to the stench. The raven flitted in and settled on a mouldy bale in the corner. Two cuckoos joined them. They each carried an egg in their beaks. The magpie also appeared. She glanced around the stable as if assessing the situation before hopping onto another bale and sizing things up with her good eye.

Nigel smiled menacingly, the episode in the woods all but forgotten. "Good work," he said in a whiny, nasal voice that seemed oddly high-pitched, even for a Scotsman. "These two should fetch a healthy sum." He took a small pouch from one pocket and placed the eggs inside, then stood and left the stable.

The raven and cuckoos hopped along behind him while Jolenta looked on in amusement. She was above begging for food. Besides, she'd already scavenged some blue-tit eggs from the hedgerows that morning.

As if remembering something, Nigel pulled out the bag containing the blackbird's remains and emptied it by the door. "Your reward. Tuck in." The gamekeeper's face then darkened and his eyes narrowed. "You'll get nothing more from me until you bring me the other falcon. I need him to make a breeding pair."

Nigel crossed the yard to a large barn and peered in through a tiny peephole. Satisfied that everything was as it should be, he entered another stable in the corner and checked the birds were still in their cage. He rubbed his hands and left the stable by a side door leading round to the back of his sprawling grey mansion. The windows were all streaked and some of the stones were loose but he wasn't concerned that it was in a state of disrepair.

He took off his dirty boots and left them next to the back door. His socks were grimy and damp and several holes in the soles were roughly sewn up. He padded across to the entrance hall, leaving outlines of his feet on the cold stone floor. He switched on his study light but the weak bulb barely lit its drab interior. He sat at an old wooden desk, picked up the phone and dialled a number. While he waited for his call to be answered he studied the stuffed animal heads mounted on the walls. A man with a deep, gruff voice eventually picked up.

Nigel shifted in his chair and prepared to thrash out the deal. "I've got three more peregrines."

"You promised me four."

"One got away," Nigel replied, his teeth clenching angrily. "If I can't catch him, you'll have to mate the young female with a falcon from the zoo."

"That's not what we agreed, Nigel," the gruff man hissed. "I need a fresh bloodline, and these migratory falcons are the best for sport. Don't back out now!"

Nigel decided to change tack. "The three I have are worth sixty thousand each."

"I don't have that much lying around."

Nigel smiled. "I take it you still want the eggs."

"Yes," said the gruff man. "Poached."

"Then find the money," Nigel said quietly. "You're guaranteeing my offer on Gordon's farm, so you can't back out of the deal either."

"How much do you want?" the voice asked.

"They're worth five thousand pounds each."

"That's a bit steep, Nigel," the gruff man said after a considered pause. "Last month you only wanted four."

"These were much harder to come by," the gamekeeper said flatly. "The price reflects that."

The gruff man took a moment to think about the offer. "I'll deposit the money in your account in the morning."

"You'll get them as soon as it's cleared," Nigel replied. "The eggs will have hatched by then."

"Deal," the gruff man said and replaced the receiver.

Nigel couldn't stand the man but, as he'd got well above

32

the going rate for the precious eggs, they had a business relationship worth nurturing. He went into the kitchen and tested the water in an old metal kettle balanced on the end of a range cooker. It was about right. A rat scurried across the floor and slipped through a crack in the wall under a sink filled with dirty pots and pans. Nigel shook his head, removed a hot water bottle from a utility cupboard and filled it. He put the eggs and bottle in a hold-all, zipped up the top and placed it on a shelf in the cupboard. Then he collected his car keys, pulled his boots back on and slipped out of the front door.

He opened the garage and climbed into an old Mercedes. A pair of huge wrought-iron gates at the bottom of a long drive opened automatically and he pulled onto the main road. Five minutes later he turned into Gordon's driveway. He parked outside the beautiful old farmhouse and switched off the engine. Pond Farm was built from faded red brick and wooden beams and had very low ceilings. Nigel was intensely jealous of his neighbour because Gordon kept the place immaculately and the grounds were also in pristine condition. He knocked on the front door and waited. Birds roosting in the trees overlooking the pond fell silent.

Gordon opened the door and wiped his mouth with a napkin. He was in the middle of dinner and didn't look pleased to see the gamekeeper because he knew what he was going to say. He decided to play the game anyway, fixing his neighbour with his emerald green eyes as if trying to mesmerise him.

"How much this time, Nigel?" he asked.

Nigel's mouth twitched and moisture formed on his top lip. "You really should accept my offer for your farm because it's extremely generous," he said, pushing forward as if trying to get Gordon to invite him in.

Gordon held up a hand. The last time Nigel had been round he'd left muddy footprints all over his new carpet.

"Let's conduct our business on the doorstep. You won't be here long enough for me to ask you in for a cup of tea."

"Very well," Nigel said irritably. "Have it your way. How does a million and a half sound?"

"It sounds fantastic," Gordon said, watching in amusement as Nigel's eyes lit up, "but it's not quite enough."

The gamekeeper's face fell. "We both know that's a lot more than this place is worth," he hissed angrily. "Why don't you just take my offer and we'll never have to see each other again?"

The farmer took a deep breath. "I've been lobbying parliament to have this land declared a nature reserve so it's not for sale."

"I saw that you'd posted MP Biggs's rejection letter on your website," Nigel said quietly.

"The man's certifiable," Gordon replied. "He wants to turn my land into battery farms. Someone has got to take a stand against clueless city boys. If I had my way I'd stick him in a cage for the rest of his life and watch him try to lay eggs."

"You can tell him that yourself this weekend," Nigel said.

Gordon frowned. "You must know something I don't."

"He's the guest speaker at the festival," Nigel explained. "Anyway, my offer still stands."

Even though he was only about five-foot-six, Gordon stood up straight and folded his arms defensively over a stomach that fought to burst from a brightly coloured waistcoat. He knew he couldn't intimidate the wiry gamekeeper but he wanted him to know that he wouldn't be threatened. "How many versions of the word 'no' don't you understand, Nigel? My family have lived at Pond Farm for three hundred years and as far as I'm concerned I'm still Lord of the Manor. No amount of bullying from you will force me to sell up and move on. So kindly take your money and insert it wherever you see fit."

Nigel looked like he'd sat on a wasp. "I want your land, Gordon. Make no mistake, I will get it eventually."

"Don't come back until you've grown up a bit," Gordon said as if talking to a small child. "If you insist on cluttering up my porch, I'll ask the dogs to see you off."

"If they come anywhere near me," Nigel spat, prodding the farmer in the chest, "I'll shoot them."

The gamekeeper stormed back to his car and accelerated hard out of Gordon's driveway, his wheels hurling gravel at the house and smashing one of the dining room windows.

5

The following morning Ryker opened his eyes and stood. He felt much better but he wasn't back to full strength just yet. He stretched his wings gingerly, mindful that the pain could return at any moment. A sharp spasm told him it would be another day or so before he'd be able to fly. It nagged at him that every minute spent at the sanctuary he could be searching for his family.

Hawkins noticed the look in his eyes. "Cheer up, Ryker. It won't be long until we're out of here."

"I can't bear sitting around doing nothing," he replied dejectedly. "I know they need me."

"There'd be no use setting you free now," Hawkins explained. "You wouldn't last a day if you couldn't escape from a fox."

Ryker knew he was right. If his wing gave out or if he became too tired to fly he'd be defenceless. "The real agony is the not knowing."

Hawkins gradually led him away from the subject, but, even when the conversation returned to his family, Ryker felt a lot better talking with a like-minded individual. He became more determined than ever to stay mentally strong, no matter what news awaited him in the outside world. During the day his wing loosened up until he could just about spread it fully.

Ryker realised that he hadn't asked Hawkins about his family. "How many of you are there at the airport?"

Hawkins looked up at the roof of his cage as if deep in thought. Every so often he would nod his head. After what seemed an unreasonably long time he said, "Four."

Ryker laughed. "Thanks for trying to cheer me up. You've a wicked sense of humour."

Just then Simone entered the recovery room with a small tray of food. She slid it into Ryker's cage. "You're going to have to get your strength up. I'm afraid I need this cage for another injured pheasant." She rearranged a couple of feed boxes and left the room.

Ryker looked across at his new friend. "It looks like I'm out of here."

"I'd get that down you pronto then," Hawkins replied.

Ryker finished the food and felt some of his strength return.

The door opened again and the vet returned with the man who had rescued him.

Gordon approached the cage. "He's looking much better."

"I'm concerned about his wing," Simone said, opening the cage and lifting Ryker out. "It's still a bit fragile and I wouldn't normally let him go for another twenty-four hours, but we've had a few more birds come in this morning and I need the room."

Gordon pointed to the other cage. "What about this poor fellow?"

"He was hit by a small plane at the airport," she replied. "He'll be here for a couple more days but he should be fine."

"So is this chap ready to be released back into the wild?" Gordon asked, tenderly stroking Ryker's back.

Simone shook her head and ran a hand through her long blonde hair. "Keep him inside in the warm overnight," she replied, easing the falcon into a lightweight travel box. "And let him go in the morning."

Gordon nodded. "What shall I do about the cat?"

Simone smiled nervously. "I forgot about her. Keep them in separate rooms. I know how much trouble she can be."

Gordon smiled and lifted the box. "Would you like to go out for dinner?"

The question caught Simone off guard and she blushed. "I didn't think you were ready."

Gordon shrugged. "I've packed all the pictures away."

"I'm busy with the festival over the weekend," she replied.

"Monday it is then," he said.

Simone gripped his hand. "I have a date Monday. Some other time perhaps."

Ryker peered through the holes in the box and flapped his good wing to attract Hawkins's attention because he mightn't see his friend for a while. "Great to meet you, Hawkins."

"You too, buddy," the kestrel said, nodding. "You know where to find me."

Ryker only just had time to say goodbye before he was carried out into the car park. The weather wasn't as nice today and the cold made his wing ache. Thankfully Gordon had the heater on in the car and the journey back to his farm was comfortable. What adventures were in store for him there, he could only guess.

When they arrived there was a van in the driveway and a man was replacing the dining room window. Gordon lifted Ryker out and took him into the kitchen. It was nice and warm in here too. The farmer filled a small water bowl and placed it in front of the box so the falcon could drink.

Ryker's throat was dry and he almost drained the bowl. It was then that he sensed danger in the kitchen. The feathers on the back of his neck ruffled up and a tingle ran along his spine. Something wasn't right, but he couldn't decide what it was. He peered through a hole at the other end of the box. He could see the edge of the table and a doorway leading into a living room opposite.

Ryker wanted to see the floor because he sensed something was under the table, but all he could make out was the top of a high-backed stool. Suddenly the stool wobbled. The tension inside the box was unbearable. Ryker knew something was stalking him, was crouching just out of sight. He could even hear short, sharp pants as it tried to control its breathing. He looked to Gordon for help but the farmer was making himself a cup of tea on the far side of the kitchen and hadn't noticed anything.

Ryker familiarised himself with the exits in case he got out of the box. Apart from one window, which was only ajar, the others were all closed. The only way out – provided he escaped the box – was straight past whatever was hunting him. Ryker clenched his talons in preparation for battle, all thoughts of finding his family shelved while he dealt with this new threat.

He glimpsed what looked like a furry whip swishing past the table end. Then it was gone. Now the stool back was wobbling again. Ryker's heart was in his mouth but there was nothing he could do. A black ball of fur suddenly leaped straight at him, but the animal landed in the water bowl and careered off the other side of the table. There was a loud crash as the bowl broke on the stone floor and water sprayed all over the kitchen. The creature screeched in surprise and bolted for the living room, where it cowered under a sofa as if ashamed of itself.

Gordon almost dropped his tea in surprise. "Blasted cat!"

The farmer opened the box and checked on Ryker. The falcon was pressed up against the far wall with his feathers spread, his mouth slightly open and his talons clenched. "Sorry about that," he said softly. "You were bound to meet Avellana sooner or later. When she sees how big and strong you are she'll leave you alone."

Gordon picked up the broken china and dropped it in a

bin in the corner. Then he lifted Ryker out of the box and carried him into the living room. "I'm sorry to have to do this now but I think you should meet face to face. That way there'll be no surprises during the night."

Ryker knew what Gordon was trying to do but reckoned it was a dangerous solution to a minor problem. Once he was back in the wild, the cat would be the least of his worries. He flapped his wings as if trying to escape but he was still weak and it was only a half-hearted effort. Gordon maintained a firm but comfortable grip around his middle so he resigned himself to the inevitable.

Gordon offered some soothing words and lowered him to face the cat. Avellana was still lurking under the sofa. Her brilliant green eyes were the only thing that betrayed her; the rest of her body blended into the darkness perfectly. She arched her back, hissed loudly, and struck out at the falcon. Ryker saw the blow coming and decided to let her know who was boss. He grabbed her paw in his beak and gave her a little nip. It was not what the cat had expected at all. She leaped in surprise and banged her head on the underside of the sofa. Twice in as many minutes she had made a fool of herself. This time she scampered back into the kitchen, leaped onto the counter and squeezed through the narrow opening in the window. Then she disappeared into the garden to sulk.

Gordon laughed heartily. "You don't mess about. She'll think twice about coming back in so you should have a quiet night. You can meet the rest of the animals in the morning."

Ryker was delighted that the cat had gone. He'd never met one before but his father had warned him about them from a young age. He could see why. They clearly didn't like birds.

*

Gordon had laid an old tea towel in the travel box and Ryker was sleeping comfortably in the cosy kitchen. He was in the middle of a dream about his family when the sound of dogs barking in the farmyard woke him. He rubbed his eyes with a wing, yawned and shook himself fully awake. It was the dead of night. A cockerel crowed in alarm, the noise almost rattling the windows. The dogs then piped up once more.

Ryker sensed something was wrong. The door to the travel case was open so he hopped out and poked his head through the window. The moon was extremely bright and bathed the yard in a silvery glow. A shadow slipped behind one of the barns opposite, and the dogs barked again. Ryker couldn't see what it was but he squeezed through onto the windowsill, spread his wings and gingerly flew to the gatepost by the yard.

The shadow crept beneath him, took cover under one of the walls and cautiously approached the chicken runs. The hens clucked in alarm and scattered. Suddenly Ryker realised what was happening. "Look out!" he shouted. "Fox!"

The animal was now clawing its way through flimsy wire to get into the henhouses. The cockerel wasn't cooped up and raced towards a stable to hide, but the fox spotted him out of the corner of its eye and gave chase. It cornered the cockerel and padded forward, licking its lips in anticipation of an easy meal. And then it pounced. The cockerel tried to leap out of its way, but the fox knocked it to the ground.

Ryker couldn't stand back and watch the cockerel get eaten so he leaped off the gatepost and swooped down to join the fray. He struck hard at the fox's head, his talons gouging furrows in its neck. The fox reared up and screeched, its paws flailing wildly. Ryker caught one in the flank and fell to the ground. The fox leaped at him but he rolled over just in time and countered with a swift kick.

The blow knocked the fox back on its haunches. It bared its teeth and collected itself, then inched forward. Ryker knew he could leap into the air to escape but he couldn't abandon the injured cockerel. He'd have to scare the fox off on his own.

The fox was wary now. Its prey wasn't helpless after all. It crossed the open ground and narrowed down Ryker's escape routes by forcing him into a corner. Help came from an unexpected quarter. The cockerel struggled to his feet and clamped his beak down hard on the fox's tail. It yelped and whirled to face him. Ryker saw his chance and leaped onto its back, pecking viciously at its exposed head.

The fox spun around and tried to shake him off, but it was no use. Ryker clung on for dear life and continued striking. Eventually the fox leaped into the air and tried to roll onto its back to crush him. Ryker jumped off and gave it a parting shot with both feet. Suitably chastised, the fox bolted for the field and leaped over the fence into the long grass.

Ryker almost collapsed with the exertion.

The cockerel inhaled deeply to catch his breath and nodded his thanks. "You saved my life," he said eventually. "I thought I was breakfast."

"I couldn't watch you get eaten," Ryker panted.

The sun was just rising above the horizon when the back door opened and Gordon appeared. He pulled on his hat and boots and grabbed his walking stick. The air outside was crisp and there was a light frost on the ground. His breath burst in small clouds that swirled and evaporated into nothingness.

He walked over to the farmyard. There was no muck on the ground – the yard was swept and washed every day by the farmhands. Although they kept one eye on the predatory falcon, the chickens clucked excitedly because they knew it was feeding time. Gordon disappeared into a stable and returned with a big bag of grain. When he'd finished pouring it into the troughs, he joined Ryker and the cockerel.

"I see you've met," he said, before nodding at the hens. "It's about time you started servicing these lovely young ladies, Eadric. You're the main man around here now that Old Tom's passed on."

The cockerel shuddered and waited for Gordon to cross the yard to the pig pen. "I'm not sure if I'm ready for this," he mumbled, eyeing up the hens, their faces in the troughs, their rears waggling in the air. "Where do you start?"

Ryker arched the feathers above one eye. "If I was you I'd have jumped in headfirst by now, especially when the farmer's encouraging you."

Eadric closed his eyes for a moment. "All in good time."

Ryker thought about pushing for an explanation but changed the subject. "Who owns all the land around here?"

"Gordon's farm sits on one edge of the Ravenswood estate," Eadric replied. "That's owned by Nigel the gamekeeper." He pecked a few grains of food from the yard, clearly relieved to be talking about something else. "He's been trying to buy this place for years but Gordon won't have any of it. We're pretty pleased about that because we've heard bad things about Nigel."

Ryker was intrigued. "Like what?"

Eadric shrugged and avoided the question. "Find Cuthbert when Gordon lets you go. He'll tell you everything."

Ryker pecked some grain and made a face. "Who's Cuthbert?"

"He's a wise old pheasant who's lived in Redlands

Forest for as long as I can remember," Eadric replied. "What he doesn't know about the North Downs isn't worth learning."

"Give me meat any day," Ryker coughed, disgusted by the grain's taste.

Eadric's tiny ears pricked up. "Now you're talking."

"Where can I find this Cuthbert?" Ryker asked.

Eadric pointed over his shoulder with his wing. "He's usually down by the stream that runs through the forest."

"How will I recognise him?" Ryker asked, thankful to be given so much information.

Eadric smiled. "He's the one with the limp."

Ryker noticed that Gordon had finished feeding the animals and collecting the chicken eggs. He hoped it was time to be released and his heart quickened. "It looks like I might be out of here, Eadric," he said. "Great talking to you."

Eadric nodded and extended his wing affectionately. "Thanks again for what you did earlier."

"You're welcome," Ryker replied. "Now, why don't you start looking after all these beautiful hens?"

Eadric gulped as if overcoming an irrational fear. "I suppose I've got to start sometime," he mumbled.

Gordon carried Ryker back to the house and placed him on the kitchen counter. He brought him some more food and water to get his strength up. While he was eating, Gordon made a quick call to the animal sanctuary. Ryker could tell by Gordon's tone and manner that Simone thought it was time for him to be released.

Gordon replaced the receiver and stroked Ryker's deep blue-grey back feathers once more. "We think you're ready for the wilds of Surrey," he said softly. "It's been nice having you around."

He picked Ryker up and took him down to the bottom

44

of the garden. On the way they passed a small plot where Gordon had buried his previous pets. The farmer stopped, bowed his head and said a quick prayer. "I'd like to take you all the way back to the nest," he said when they reached the stile, "but I've got work to do. The exercise will do you good."

Ryker rubbed his head against Gordon's shoulder as if thanking him for his kindness. Then he spread his wings, flapped hard and leaped into the air. The sense of freedom was exhilarating. He swooped low over Gordon before climbing steeply and heading across the field to the nests. The farmer watched him closely to see how his wing was faring. The falcon slightly favoured one side but that was only to be expected after the injury.

The last of the joint's stiffness soon eased and Ryker found he could execute all the sharp turns and steep dives required for survival. He spotted his nest and raced towards the cliff, but there was no movement. His heart raced but his expectation fell. He flared his wings and landed on the cliff face, his optimism fading and his mood deepening.

The remains of the nest were scattered across the ledge. Stained feathers clinging to the steep chalk walls told him that the fight had been bitter and bloody. It didn't look good. He searched for clues but soon gave up. There was no sign of Safiyya or the eggs. Ryker's head started to spin and he almost broke down. He knew there was no point staying so he flew along the cliff to his parents' nest.

There were more signs of battle here. Three dead cuckoos lined the scrape and a couple of ravens lay on the path below. Algar must have put up a spirited fight, but to find no sign of them was devastating. In one morning he'd lost his entire family. Ryker collapsed onto the ledge and wept.

How long he stayed there he couldn't tell but it must have been several hours because when he eventually wiped away the last of his tears it was dusk. Fighting off a feeling of despair, and believing deep inside that one or more of them were alive, Ryker steeled himself for a long journey of discovery. Brushing all thoughts of personal safety aside, he knew exactly where to start.

He looked over the nests one last time to be sure he hadn't missed anything. He briefly thought about following the trail of dead cuckoos but the battle had been confined to the cliffs and the field and it lead nowhere. He took a deep breath and headed for the stream a mile away. He soon spotted a well-fed chestnut-brown pheasant where the brook entered the forest.

Ryker dropped out of the sky like a stone and landed on a branch above the oblivious bird. "Excuse me," he called down, "but can you tell me where I can find Cuthbert?"

The pheasant carried on searching for food as if Ryker didn't exist, so he called again, only louder this time. The pheasant cocked its head as if trying to make something out, then shook it and continued strutting through the long grass.

Ryker shrugged and jumped down to join the pheasant. He landed behind it and bellowed, "Cuthbert?!"

The pheasant leaped in startled surprise and almost collapsed. "By God, have you no manners, young man?"

Now it was Ryker's turn to look shocked. "I called out but you ignored me."

Falcons were a natural enemy and couldn't be trusted so the pheasant backed off. "I'm a little deaf."

"Are you Cuthbert?"

The pheasant had to read Ryker's beak, but he understood every word. "Good heavens, no. I'm his brother Wilbur."

"Apparently Cuthbert knows everything that goes on around here," Ryker said hopefully.

"Does he now," Wilbur said evenly.

"I think my family were taken to the Ravenswood estate after the fight on the cliffs," Ryker added. "I have to find them."

"Sinnie tried to warn you about those ravens but you wouldn't listen," Wilbur said. "She risked her life to come up to your nests."

"That was my father's fault," Ryker said disconsolately. "He shooed her away before she could tell us what she'd heard."

Wilbur shook his head. "You can't go around blaming others for your own shortcomings. Help was offered but you refused it." A drop of rain landed between them and Wilbur glanced at the gathering clouds. "There's a storm coming," he said, returning to his foraging. "I'm stocking up on supplies, so you'll have to excuse me." He turned his back on Ryker and marched into the forest, leaving a confused and fearful falcon alone in the field.

Ryker couldn't understand why he didn't want to help. It hadn't dawned on him that his father's fearsome reputation was to blame and that the local birds had a deep-seated hatred of the haughty falcons. The fact that Algar made no discrimination between them when hunting for food didn't help either.

The wind picked up and the rain came down. Ryker shook the water out of his feathers and flew back to the nest. He landed on the ledge, curled up in the remains of the scrape and wept again.

Sometime during the evening he was roused by another disturbance. This time it was coming from Redlands Forest. His father had taught him the many sounds and smells of the forest and he recognised it as the distress call of a pheasant. Ryker covered his ears and tried to get some sleep, but it was no use. The calls were getting louder. A second pheasant joined in, helping create an almighty din.

Ryker was torn between staying where he was and

investigating. The longer he thought about it, the easier his decision became. If he could help the pheasants, maybe they would take him under their wings. With his confidence at rock bottom, and nowhere left to turn, he leaped off the cliff and flew down to the stream.

There was a faint path through the trees, which he just managed to navigate in the fading light. He followed the track towards the distress calls but the branches eventually became so thick that he had to land and find his way through the bracken and fallen trees on the forest floor on foot. The commotion was just up ahead.

He finally rounded an enormous tree stump and entered a clearing. Two pheasants were cowering under a low branch opposite while a fox tried to prise them out with its paw. She managed to grab one by the tail and dragged it into the clearing to feast. The pheasant screeched in terror.

Ryker knew what had to be done, so he marched into the clearing and coughed quietly.

The fox released the pheasant and whirled to face him. "You again!" she hissed.

Wilbur picked himself up and rejoined his brother under the tree. "Thank the Lord you're here."

Ryker couldn't help himself. "Your knight in shining armour, I'm not," he said, dismissing Wilbur with a look and concentrating on the furry mass of anger and claws in front of him. "Why can't you leave us alone?"

The fox fixed him with a steady glare. "A girl's got to eat, but every time I try to grab a meal, you show up."

Ryker shrugged. "There are plenty of sheep on Nigel's farm."

"And risk that shotgun?" the fox scoffed. "He killed my father with it. Then his rabid dog took my mother on one of his illegal hunts."

A plan formed in the back of Ryker's mind. "If you hate him so much, why don't you join us?"

48

The fox shook her head. "I'll leave you alone tonight but if I can't find anything to eat I'll be back in the morning."

Ryker spread his wings and lunged forward. "I'll be waiting," he said as if overcome with irrational bravado. He was absolutely terrified and if the fox had countered he'd have been in deep trouble. Thankfully it fell for his bluff and disappeared into the forest. Ryker's wobbly legs gave out and he sagged to the ground.

Cuthbert peered out from under the fallen tree and approached cautiously. His green neck feathers were even more vivid than his brother's and his limp was quite pronounced. He helped Ryker back to his feet and showed him into their nest. "Thank you, kind sir. That was very brave."

"I don't think I'd have made round two," Ryker mumbled.

Wilbur welcomed them in. "My brother Cuthbert."

Cuthbert looked confused. "You two know each other?"

Ryker couldn't bring himself to face Wilbur. "I asked him about the fight on the cliffs but he claimed not to know anything and didn't want to help."

Cuthbert smiled and patted Ryker on the shoulder. "How quickly times change, eh, brother?"

Wilbur coughed and spluttered and looked sheepishly at the ground.

Ryker decided to change the subject to avoid a family dispute. And he tried to put them at ease with his friendly manner so that they'd tell him everything. "Gordon's cockerel said you knew more about the estate than anyone else. He also said you might know why the ravens and cuckoos attacked my nest."

"So you've met Eadric," Cuthbert said. "Poor confused creature. I think he's going through a phase." He drank from a knot in the wood that had collected some of the earlier rainwater. "We've been here nearly all my adult life. We've made every effort with your father, but he still won't have anything to do with us."

Ryker nodded. "He's quite set in his ways."

"It's time you learned that we Redlands birds must stick together if we want to stop the ravens and cuckoos terrorising the forest."

This was the opening Ryker had been waiting for. "Well I'm willing to listen, even if he wasn't."

Cuthbert had his own agenda of course. He'd been trying to rid the forest of the evil ravens for years but he'd never had a powerful enough ally. Ryker might be that ally so it'd be best to keep him onside. "Nigel the gamekeeper owns the estate," Cuthbert explained. "He runs a battery farm for his chickens and keeps other livestock in the fields. I've heard he treats his animals like, well, you know. And he's not shy with his shotgun either."

"Is that how you got the limp?" Ryker asked.

Cuthbert shook his head. "No, I got this a long time ago in the Highlands. A hunter was about to take a pot shot at a friend. I distracted him and took the bullet. Hurts in winter, I can tell you."

Ryker was desperate to learn more about the fight on the cliffs. "Did you see what happened to my family?"

Cuthbert nodded. "After you fell, the ravens forced your mate out of the nest so the cuckoos could take your eggs. They probably brought them back to Nigel for him to sell."

Ryker choked back the tears again. "What about my parents?"

"They were alive when I last saw them," Cuthbert said encouragingly. "But they were overwhelmed by the ravens and taken to the estate. Don't even think of going up there. Get past the electric fence and you'll run into the dog. No one's ever managed it."

"Can't we fly in?"

Cuthbert shook his head. "The skies above the wood are patrolled by Dillon, a raven with a mean streak and foul temper. Cross him at your peril."

"How come you know so much about the place?" Ryker asked.

"He used to breed homing pigeons," Cuthbert replied. "The conditions were apparently so awful that a number tried to escape. Whether by luck or judgement – I suspect luck, as will you once you've met him – one managed to get out and spread the word about Nigel and his farm."

"Who's the brave escapee?" Ryker asked.

"Hatcher," Cuthbert replied, "the now homeless homing pigeon. No wonder he has been known to fly around in confused circles."

"Can I meet him?" Ryker asked.

Cuthbert nodded. "It's late, but he might still be up. Follow me."

6

Ryker bid Wilbur goodbye and followed Cuthbert further into the woods. He rarely scoured the forest floor and all the new sights and sounds and smells intrigued him. After about ten minutes Cuthbert stopped beneath a large oak tree. It was raining again and the drops made a rhythmic pattering on the new leaves.

Cuthbert called up to Hatcher's nest, which was carefully hidden in a fork between three large branches. "Can you spare a moment, mon ami?"

A few seconds passed before a head peered out of the nest, looked around as if in a daze and then retreated back into the nest.

Cuthbert shook his head in mock exasperation. "There are at least three dimensions, Hatcher. Try looking down."

The pigeon poked his head out again and spotted the pheasant. "Oh, hello, Cuthbert," he said in a thick Welsh accent. "How are you?"

"Mellowing with age."

Hatcher frowned. "I didn't know you had jaundice. You'd better come up."

"I've brought a friend," Cuthbert replied, wondering what on earth the pigeon was talking about.

Hatcher clearly couldn't see Ryker in the fading light. "Well ask him to join us," he said.

Cuthbert nodded to the falcon and they both leaped into the air. Ryker was far more agile than the old pheasant – who had to circle the tree twice – and he landed on the bough before him.

Hatcher, who had been sitting calmly in his nest with his

mate, suddenly jumped up and down yelling hysterically. "You've turned into a falcon, Cuthbert, a blooming great falcon! Help!"

Cuthbert landed a moment later and gave the pigeon a friendly squeeze on the shoulder. "Don't worry, Hatcher. This is Ryker, the friend I was just telling you about."

"I knew that," Hatcher said sheepishly. "I was just letting him know who's in charge."

"Of course you were," Cuthbert said, humouring him. "Can't you see he's petrified?" He gave Ryker a knowing look.

Ryker took his cue and trembled in mock terror. "Sorry to disturb you, Hatcher," he said nervously, "but I'd like to pick your brain."

"What for?" Hatcher asked excitedly. "A prize?"

"Unlikely," Cuthbert muttered under his breath.

Hatcher rediscovered his customary bluster. "Well, come in, come in."

Thick branches offered protection from the wind and a canopy of leaves kept the rain at bay. It was dark now and the birds had to strain to see each other, although the slow rise of the moon did give them some background light. A couple of bats flitted through the trees emitting their high-pitched squeaks. Ryker was hungry and knew they made a tasty snack but he ignored them.

Cuthbert shifted his rear onto a knot in one branch. "We need to know all you can tell us about Nigel's farm."

Hatcher cast his mind back to his time in Ravenswood and shuddered. "It was a horrible place, Cuthbert. Nigel had us cooped up in tiny cages for most of the day. We were given starvation rations and made to work extremely hard. Quite a few of the birds died."

"How did you escape?" Ryker asked.

Hatcher looked around nervously. "These walls have ears. Join me in my office."

Cuthbert and Ryker had no idea what he was talking

about but they followed him up to another crook anyway.

"The gamekeeper enters a number of events each year," Hatcher said when they'd made themselves comfortable. "The last one was a homing pigeon race from farms across central England back to Ravenswood. We made up our minds to try to escape during the race but Nigel had other ideas and tagged us so he could find us. It was only by good fortune that I got lost and was attacked by a hawk. My tag came off in the struggle, the hawk gave up and I was free. Some of the other pigeons thought they could run anyway but Nigel tracked them down and shot them."

Ryker shook his head in disbelief. "You must have thought you'd had it when you got attacked, but the hawk actually ended up saving you."

"That's why you startled me earlier," Hatcher said, nodding. "You see us pigeons as easy targets."

"What more can you tell us?" Ryker asked, changing the subject because his stomach was rumbling.

"Nigel runs the place with heavy hands," Hatcher said quietly, as if someone else was trying to listen in. "He thinks nothing of sending his livestock off to slaughter well before their time if they get on the wrong side of him."

"How many animals does he have up there?" Cuthbert asked.

"At least a hundred sheep, and probably the same number of cattle," Hatcher replied. "Add them together and you get..." He cocked his head. "Well, you get lots. They graze the fields during the day but they're locked up in cramped barns overnight. He also keeps twenty pigs in a tiny sty in the yard and a couple of dozen homing pigeons next door. There were more outbuildings but we weren't allowed near them."

Cuthbert scratched an itch under his chin with his foot. "It's too dangerous to scout the farm with Dillon and his

54

enforcers out on patrol."

"Perhaps we could find out to whom Nigel's been selling the eggs," Ryker suggested.

"Oh, I can help you there," Hatcher said. "He sends lots of birds to the Feathered-Friends Park."

"It's a huge avian zoo a hundred miles away," Cuthbert explained. He could only imagine what this was doing to Ryker and offered his wing as comfort. "I've heard about it happening with other species but don't take it as gospel."

"I need to get to this park," Ryker said resolutely, his insides churning. He inhaled slowly to keep his emotions in check. "If they're there, I'll find them."

Cuthbert nodded. "Hatcher can guide you. I'm not strong enough to fly that far and neither is my brother, but I might know someone on the inside who can help."

"Who?" Ryker asked.

"Let me speak to my brother first," Cuthbert replied.

"We can leave in the morning," Ryker said.

Cuthbert smiled. "Patience is a virtue."

The birds climbed down to Hatcher's nest where his mate was waiting.

Ryker looked at his feet as Hatcher made the introductions. "I'm so sorry we didn't listen to you."

Sinnie shrugged. "Apology accepted. It's your loss."

Cuthbert and Ryker were about to leave when one of Hatcher's chicks piped up angrily. "I'm hungry, Dad. Where's my dinner?"

Hatcher turned to his son. "I'm busy, boyo. Give me a couple of minutes."

The chick shook his head. "I want my dinner now. It's dark and I'm tired. I need to eat before I go to bed."

Something about the exchange puzzled Cuthbert. He'd seen Hatcher a few days earlier and his two chicks had been extremely polite, if a little dippy. "He's not normally like this, is he?" he asked.

Hatcher shook his head. "I don't know what's brought it on."

Cuthbert hadn't paid the chicks any attention until now but as he ushered the pigeon aside his mouth fell. "Good grief, Hatcher," he spluttered. "Have you not noticed anything odd about your chicks?"

Now it was Hatcher's turn to look puzzled. "Not really. Only that this one appeared from nowhere, then changed colour and grew four times bigger."

"And you didn't find that strange!" Cuthbert gasped.

"This is my first time at fatherhood, Cuthbert," Hatcher said with a shrug. "I thought he was eating a bit more."

The pheasant shook his head in disbelief. "Hatcher, you had two chicks of your own. Now you have three. The third is a cuckoo chick. You must get rid of him now to have any chance of raising the others!"

"What?" Sinnie said. "You want us to disown him?"

Cuthbert was becoming exasperated. "This bird is a spy. He'll kill your chicks if you carry on feeding him. He's a parasite, an evil, wicked leech."

"Well, if you put it like that, I guess we have no choice," Hatcher said disconsolately. "Shame. I rather liked him."

Cuthbert looked at Ryker. "Do the honours please."

Ryker didn't know if he could bring himself to kill a young bird, but the more he thought about what this chick's family had done to his, the easier the decision became. "What's the best way?"

"Push him out of the nest," Cuthbert replied. "He won't last the night on the forest floor."

"You wouldn't dare," the cuckoo screeched. "I own this nest. I belong here."

Ryker cut him off with a look that could shred flesh. "You don't belong in Redlands Forest." He grasped the cuckoo round the neck and threw him out of the tree. "Enjoy your flight."

The chick landed with a dull thud.

Cuthbert gripped Hatcher by the shoulders. "They're trying to take over the forest. Spread the word, and be on the lookout for more of them. See you in the morning."

The birds didn't notice a cuckoo watching them from a branch close by. Flint floated silently to the ground and checked his chick was okay. As Ryker followed Cuthbert up the faint path and disappeared into thick foliage, he smiled and whispered a single word: "Gotcha!"

7

Their night vision wasn't good enough for them to fly through the trees back to the nest, so Ryker followed Cuthbert up the faint path on the forest floor. He had no idea how the pheasant found his way in near total darkness but guessed the wily old bird knew the route by heart having lived here most of his life.

Cuthbert stopped just before they reached the clearing and rapped his beak on a fallen tree. The trunk was hollow and the noise echoed eerily. "Just to let Wilbur know that it's friend rather than foe," he said, winking. "He claims he can't hear very well but you'd be surprised."

Wilbur was snoring when they entered the nest but he opened one eye when they joined him. He nodded a tired greeting and was snoring again within a minute.

Ryker took Cuthbert up on his offer of a bed, but he didn't manage much sleep. He was troubled by what Nigel had done with his family and the night dragged on interminably. His relationship with his father had always been difficult but the bond between them was still strong.

Eventually he sat up. The pheasants were sound asleep. Despite their dire warnings, he had to find out what went on at Nigel's. He crept out of the nest, tiptoed across the clearing and used the moonlight to guide him back to the stream where the trees weren't quite as thick. The forest above was deathly quiet, and a deep sense of loneliness threatened to overwhelm him.

He gazed across the field at the dark and mysterious Ravenswood opposite. It seemed oddly menacing, which contrasted completely with Redlands. He took a deep breath and shivered. His mind made up, he leaped into the air and flew low across the field into the unknown. He didn't notice a cuckoo drop from the branches behind him and follow at a safe distance.

Ryker landed on a branch overhanging the fence. He wondered what the low-pitched humming was but noticed it came from a large white box mounted about halfway up. He checked the trees and gulped when he saw how many raven nests there were. The pheasants had been right: this was a minefield. He hoped their roosting would drown out the noise of his wings as he flitted from branch to branch before dropping down to a faint path through the woods. He stole a glance over his shoulder and crept towards the gamekeeper's farm.

Flint landed on a branch above the path and tapped the edge of a nest with his beak. "You need to see this," he whispered.

Dillon poked his head out and followed Flint's gaze. "Like a lamb to the slaughter," he said smugly as the falcon crossed a sliver of moonlight. "With him out of the way, all this will be mine. Rouse the flock."

Ryker cocked his head every so often to listen for trouble but nothing seemed out of the ordinary and he soon reached Nigel's yard. It was quiet, save for the wind rustling in the trees. He leaped onto the windowsill of the nearest barn and peered inside. There were cages of all shapes and sizes holding different bird species, several of which Ryker didn't recognise. Only a few were empty. The window was open a fraction of an inch. Ryker hooked it with his foot and pulled, then slipped through the gap and dropped onto the floor.

Some of the birds seemed curious, while others shook their heads as if trying to warn him. Ryker ignored them and flew along the aisles hoping to find his family. There was no sign of them. He stopped by an owl's cage and bowed his head.

"You're either brave or stupid," the owl said suddenly, "or both. Pass me the keys on that hook."

Ryker noticed that the owl's perfect woodland camouflage was spoiled by a vivid tuft of pure white feathers in the centre of his chest. He couldn't place his accent but knew he must have travelled a long way from home. "Which one?"

"The bunch by the door," the owl said impatiently. "Come on. We haven't got all night. Nigel often wanders round late and you never know where Dillon is."

Ryker grabbed the keys from the hook by the barn door and passed them through the bars. "The raven?"

The owl selected a key with his foot, slid it into the lock and the cage opened noiselessly. "A nasty piece of work."

Some of the other birds were now taking a keen interest in the pair. Ryker looked them over. "Shouldn't we release them?"

The owl shook his head. "There's not enough time to free them all, so how do you decide which ones to let go?" He closed his cage door and dropped the keys onto the hook. "You can come back for them another time." He leaped onto the windowsill and slipped out into the night.

Ryker had no option but to follow, the long faces of the other birds in the barn nagging at his conscience. "What do you know about Dillon?"

The owl drew his wing across his throat. "Keep it down!" he hissed. "That'll have to wait. We need to get out of here."

"Please!" Ryker begged. "I helped you escape."

The owl couldn't hide his exasperation. "Originally there were only cuckoos here," he whispered. "When Dillon turned up staking a claim to the wood they tried to force him out of his nest, but the raven fought back. The cuckoos couldn't defeat him so he became their leader by default, and that's when his flock moved in. The two sides don't like each other but, as they both work for Nigel, they put up with the arrangement."

"They took my family," Ryker said quietly.

The owl suddenly understood his desperation and cocked his head towards a barn opposite. "Try in there first, then work your way round."

"Will you show me?" Ryker pleaded.

The owl shook his head. "I've done my bit. I've been cooped up here way too long. See you around." He bent his legs, leaped off the sill and disappeared into the night.

Ryker immediately felt vulnerable but there was no point staying where he was. He checked the yard and flew across to the other barn, a deep sense of dread filling him. He landed on the windowsill and looked inside. Somewhere in the grounds a dog barked. Ryker almost jumped out of his skin and froze, blood roaring in his ears. He stood like a statue for a minute before exhaling. False alarm.

The barn was crammed with rows of battery chickens in tiny cages. They looked frail, undernourished, miserable. Ryker shook his head and flitted across to the next outbuilding. His heart skipped a beat when he saw his father in a cage on the far side. He tried the window but it was locked. He was just about to rap on the glass to attract his attention when he heard a noise behind him. He whirled round, fear rising in his stomach. Dillon was standing on the roof above him.

The raven opened and closed his scarred beak in evil anticipation, a sadistic glint in his charcoal eyes. "Well, well, look who's here!"

A fork of lightning pierced the clouds above the cliffs and illuminated a huge flock of ravens on the roof opposite. They had already recaptured the owl and held him securely in their grip. Thunder rumbled ominously in the distance but the clouds parted and bathed Ryker in the moonlight. He looked for an escape route but he was surrounded.

The owl shrugged. "Tried to warn you, buddy."

"Seize him!" Dillon cried.

Four ravens leaped off the roof and scythed in at Ryker. They spread their wings and clenched their talons as they drew closer, and he could hear them hissing angrily. He had a split second to react, and knew that if he wanted to save his family, he couldn't afford to be captured.

Ryker reared up to show them how big and strong he was before leaping straight at them. The boldness of his attack surprised them and two wisely veered off. But Ryker struck hard at the others, drawing blood with a fierce double swipe of his talons. The ravens screeched in pain and retreated.

"Take him now!" Dillon roared.

Ryker ignored the cowardly raven, who only seemed to want to delegate. Instead, he spun on his tail and took careful aim at the ravens holding the owl. They didn't have time to get out of his way and he knocked them both aside.

As they tumbled into the mud, the owl looked at him and smiled. "Let's get the flock out of here!"

Ryker was disoriented so he fell in behind the owl and raced across the yard into the trees. The squawking that erupted behind them told him the ravens were hot on their heels.

"Don't let them escape!" Dillon bellowed.

Ryker found it difficult to follow the owl because he was extremely manoeuvrable. He flitted among the branches as if he had a sixth sense and it was all Ryker could do to keep up.

"They can't see in the dark," the owl called over his shoulder.

"Neither can I," Ryker gasped, dipping under a branch

that almost took his head off.

"Stick to me like glue," the owl replied with a wink.

Ryker concentrated on keeping the owl's tail dead ahead but it wasn't easy. Trees flashed past in the moonlight, branches reaching out to knock him down. He could hear the ravens getting closer and glanced over his shoulder. He could just make out a pair of vivid yellow eyes closing in fast. He checked on the owl and made a sharp turn to avoid a thick bough. He heard a crunch behind him as the raven missed the turn and ploughed headlong into the tree. One down!

Ryker checked his tail once more. Dillon cut past the other ravens and took the lead in the chase. He knew every tree in the forest and wouldn't be shaken off. Ryker redoubled his efforts and accelerated towards the field hoping that the raven wouldn't follow them if they made it into Redlands Forest.

As they approached the fence an enormous oak appeared. "Split!" the owl shouted over his shoulder.

Ryker understood immediately and the birds separated. Dillon was caught in two minds for a moment and it cost him. He started to go after the owl before remembering how important the falcon was to Nigel. By the time he'd positioned himself for a strike it was too late. He careered headlong into the oak, his beak penetrating an inch into the bark, the vibration running the length of his body.

He couldn't swear because his beak was embedded so deep in the tree that he couldn't open it. He braced his wings against the oak and pushed with all his might. His beak suddenly popped free and he tumbled to the ground, landing with a heavy bump. He dusted himself down and glared after the fleeing birds.

"Your freedom will come at a price," he hissed.

Ryker laughed out loud when he heard the thud. He

rejoined the owl and they headed across the field. The remaining ravens gave up the chase to check on Dillon so, for now, they were in the clear.

Ryker drew alongside as they approached Redlands Forest. "Now it's your turn to follow me."

The owl let Ryker take the lead and the falcon cut into the trees by the stream. They flew as far as possible before landing and walking the faint path to the clearing. They eventually tiptoed across to the pheasants' nest.

Cuthbert's eyes flicked open. "Where have you been, young man?"

Ryker could have lied but the pheasant would see straight through him. "Nigel's."

Cuthbert shook his head. "I told you not to go up there. Remember what I said about working together? That means looking out for each other too, you know."

Wilbur stirred and rolled onto his feet. "Won't you introduce us?"

Ryker shrugged. "I'm ashamed to admit it, but I don't know his name."

The owl stepped forward, drew his wing across his chest like a cape and bowed deeply. "Naz. Tawny Owl."

"So what's your story?" Cuthbert asked.

"I won't bore you with the autobiography," the owl replied. "But the condensed version reads like this: I escaped from the Feathered-Friends Zoo a couple of years ago. On my way home I got caught in one of Nigel's traps."

Cuthbert nodded thoughtfully. "You need to go back."

The owl laughed off his suggestion as ridiculous. "There's a raven after my blood. Forget it."

Cuthbert shook his head. "I meant to the zoo."

"Please, Naz," Ryker said. "I think my wife has been taken there."

Naz held up a wing, took a few paces backwards and waved. "They'll lock me up again. Thanks but no thanks."

Cuthbert drew Ryker close. "I have a confession to make. I know Safiyya might be at the zoo, but that's not the only reason I want you to go. An old Highland friend owes me a favour, and I think he might be there too. You, Hatcher and Naz might be able to release him. He's getting on a bit but he'd still be a useful ally in our disagreement with the ravens."

Naz continued backing away. "This sounds far too dangerous. I've got a home to get to and it's halfway round the world."

"If you don't help us," Cuthbert said sternly, "Dillon and his cohorts will overrun the forest. It's lose-lose for us."

"This isn't my home or my problem," Naz countered. "Besides, I escaped a long time ago. I don't know the way back."

"We have a homing pigeon to guide us," Ryker said.

"Come on, we're even," Naz said. "And why should I take all the risks?"

Cuthbert nodded slowly and retreated into the nest. "I'm sorry, you're right. You've no reason to help us. Have a safe trip."

"But, Cuthbert," said Ryker, "we need him. He's got great night vision and knows how to fight."

"Let him go, Ryker," Cuthbert said firmly. "Goodbye, Naz."

Ryker watched the owl disappear into the forest with a touch of sadness. He knew Naz could have helped them and it upset him that he didn't want anything to do with their struggle against the ravens.

"There are still a few hours before daybreak," Cuthbert said. "You've had a long night and must be tired. Try to get some rest."

Ryker took one last look after the owl before settling into the soft leaves under the fallen tree. Cuthbert was snoring within minutes but Ryker's mind was still swirling uncontrollably. There were too many questions and not enough answers, but eventually his brain could take no more and he slipped into a troubled sleep.

He'd hardly dropped off when he woke again with a start.

Something was creeping into the clearing. Ryker's senses were suddenly on full alert but the clouds had closed in and he couldn't see a thing. He strained his ears and heard the faint crunch of feet on the leaf litter. Whatever it was, it was crossing the clearing as quietly as possible. Ryker couldn't believe Dillon would be so stupid but that meant facing an unknown intruder.

He slipped out from underneath the tree to meet the danger head on. If it was the fox, he'd try to surprise it. His heart was thumping in his chest. He felt cold and clammy, a bundle of nerves. A twig snapped; the noise deafening.

And then the moon popped out for a brief moment. Ryker spotted a shadow a few feet to his right and leaped at it. It was a move borne from his own terror, but he hoped it would scare off the intruder. The shadow leaped backwards and Ryker fell flat on his face.

"You forget that I can see in the dark," Naz said quietly, helping Ryker to his feet.

Ryker trembled with adrenalin. "You frightened the life out of me!" he whispered.

Naz smiled. "Sorry. I didn't want to wake you. You'd better count me in."

Ryker frowned. "Why the change of heart?"

Naz shrugged. "If the truth be told, I haven't got many friends."

Ryker now understood why Cuthbert had dismissed him with such short thrift. The wily pheasant had seen through Naz's blustery exterior and knew that a blunt but polite send-off would play on the owl's conscience.

Ryker welcomed him into the nest. "I think you just

made some. Now, let's get some sleep."

"Spoken like an owl, bro'," Naz whispered. "Spoken like an owl."

8

The first rays of dawn cast shadows across the nest. The overnight rain had cleared and the wind had dropped. It was going to be a glorious day. Ryker stirred and rolled over. Naz was already stretching his wings and shaking his head to clear it of sleep.

Cuthbert stuck his beak into the tree trunk and dug out a pile of juicy worms and grubs. "Breakfast is served."

Ryker ate his fill and drank from a hollowed-out piece of wood that had collected rainwater during the night. A rustling in the bushes had him preparing for another confrontation but it was only Hatcher.

The pigeon took one look at Naz and clapped his wings together. "Alright, we've recruited a barn owl too!"

Naz gave him a strange look. "I'm tawny."

"A Geordie?" Hatcher replied, surprised. "Whey-hi, Tony."

Naz shook his head and sighed. "One of the villages round here must be an idiot short. You could have warned me."

Ryker laughed. "Then you might not have come!"

"It's time," Cuthbert said.

"Thank you for your help," Ryker said. "I'm glad I met you."

Wilbur stood to attention, his chest thrust out as if expecting a medal to be pinned on it. "And you too, sir. Godspeed."

"You know what to do when you get there," Cuthbert said. "I'd love to be going with you but at my age..."

Ryker picked up the sadness in his voice and tried to

understand what it must be like to grow old. He guessed that Cuthbert had once been young and powerful and was perhaps finding it hard to accept his advancing years. He looked the others over, a nervous anticipation building in his stomach. "Set a course for Feathered-Friends – a place that sounds like it doesn't live up to its name."

Cuthbert took them to the edge of the field and patted Ryker on the back. "I know this is hard for you but it's time to show your inner strength. You must believe they're still alive. I do."

"I know my dad is," Ryker said, his face set. "He can take care of himself. It's the others I'm worried about."

The farewells made, Ryker followed Hatcher and Naz into the air. Hatcher circled the forest muttering 'Feathered-Friends, Feathered-Friends' to himself as he searched for the right direction. Ryker and Naz exchanged looks suggesting they weren't confident in their guide but they fell in behind Hatcher anyway. The homing pigeon eventually got his bearings and set off south. Not having any idea where the zoo was, the others fanned out in his slipstream.

After about fifteen minutes Hatcher looked around as if lost.

Ryker drew alongside. "Everything okay?"

"I think we might have taken a wrong turn a while back," Hatcher replied seriously, not realising how silly he sounded. "I don't recognise the ground below."

Ryker arched the feathers above one eye. "Have you been to the Feathered-Friends Park before?"

Hatcher shook his head.

Ryker couldn't believe it. "Well if you haven't been there, how would you know what it looks like?"

Hatcher shrugged. "I thought I'd have some idea."

Ryker began to understand that because Hatcher didn't have a permanent home, his homing instincts and sense of direction perhaps weren't as sharp as they should be.

He was about to say something to that effect when a loud roar startled them. A huge aeroplane thundered out from behind a solitary puff of brilliant white cloud. Naz was caught out and tumbled end over end in its slipstream. He finally righted himself and rejoined the others as the plane's wheels kissed a runway in the distance.

"Could I get a two-second warning next time?" Naz asked sarcastically.

Hatcher nodded. "If you think it'll help."

Ryker suddenly realised where they were. "Naz, take Hatcher down. I'll meet you in the fields in a minute."

"Where are you going?" the owl asked in his strange accent.

"To find a friend," Ryker replied mysteriously.

Ryker flew into the flight-path, hoping that his friend was on duty and had seen him. He didn't have to wait long. He was about a quarter of a mile from the runway when a pair of birds came barrelling towards him at high speed. Ryker smiled broadly when he noticed one of them was missing a leg. "Back in the air I see!"

"I wondered why a falcon was being so foolish as to cross the flight-path," the kestrel said, a welcoming glint in his eyes. "What brings you here?"

Ryker followed them out of harm's way. "We're on our way to the Feathered-Friends Park, but I think our guide got a little lost."

Hawkins frowned. "A little! I heard the park was way out west." He turned to his partner. "Don't worry, Asketil, I'll take it from here."

"You got it," Asketil said, peeling off and heading back to his hide at the end of the runway.

Hawkins dropped towards the field, his tone turning serious. "Why do you want to go to the zoo?"

Ryker landed next to Hatcher and Naz and made the introductions. "We think the gamekeeper might be selling eggs to the park."

Hawkins took a deep breath. "I want to help."

"But you have a job and a family here," Ryker replied.

Hawkins shrugged, his mind made up. "The life of a friend is equally important. They'll understand. Besides, I haven't been able to do the job properly since I got back because I'm too jumpy. Let me clear it with Asketil and the wife." He didn't give Ryker time to argue and leaped into the air. Within five minutes he was back. "Okay, I just resigned."

"From marriage?" Hatcher muttered. "I didn't know you could do that."

Hawkins cocked his head at an oblivious Hatcher. "Is he okay?"

Ryker put his wing to his mouth and gestured for Hawkins not to take it any further. "Don't ask. It'll only confuse him."

Naz stretched to his full height and extended his wings. "It feels like we're the four musketeers."

They followed Hatcher into the air and waited until he had his bearings. "We need to go northwest," he said eventually. "Does anyone know which way that is?"

"Due west would be better," Hawkins said, turning to his left. "The zoo is out beyond the ancient stones."

"Normally you'd be right," Hatcher replied, "but the breeze will blow us off course unless we compensate."

"The wind is blowing from the southwest," Naz countered.

"Precisely," Hatcher said. "You're getting the hang of this navigation thing a lot quicker than I did."

"I can't wait 'til the stars are out," Naz muttered. "Then we won't have to follow Captain 'Sense of Direction'."

Whatever their misgivings about Hatcher's route, the first half hour was positively peaceful. They were heading into the unknown, and things might get dangerous, but for now they were able to relax and enjoy the morning sun on their backs and a fresh breeze in their faces.

Ryker's insides were still churning. He had so much riding on their success that he had to clench his talons to fight a rising anger in his chest. Nigel had to pay for what he'd done.

As midday approached, and the birds had just swapped positions for the third time to give the leader a rest, a new horizon appeared. Instead of rolling fields interspersed with the odd copse of trees and small settlement, a vast grey jungle loomed. More buildings cluttered the landscape and replaced all the greenery. There was noise from hundreds of cars and their fumes blanketed the area in a light haze.

Naz drew alongside Hatcher. "Either we're in the wrong place or the park has expanded."

Hatcher looked puzzled. "It does seem a bit big, doesn't it?"

"A bit!" Naz exclaimed. "It started off as a twenty-acre site near the Pillars of the Sun, the old stone monument worshipped by the humans. That's not even as big as one of Gordon's fields. This is different. This is a city. This, dear travellers, is London."

"Really?" Hatcher said, clearly surprised. "I didn't think London looked like this."

"Have you been to London before?" Hawkins asked.

"Umm, no," Hatcher said after a three-second pause. "But it can't be. I plotted the route in my head. We must be a long way east of where we are."

Naz screwed up his face as he tried to work out what Hatcher meant. "Why don't we meet on the ledge of that clock-tower? I'm sure we could all do with a rest."

After they'd landed, Hatcher traced a route on the ledge with the tip of his wing as if trying to work out what had gone wrong. He shook his head and muttered something about disruptions to his magnetic field. He was so engrossed that he didn't hear a loud click from the clock.

The other three covered their ears with their wings.

"What's going on?" Hatcher asked. When they didn't reply, he huffed, "Okay, I give up."

A deafening 'BONG!' cut him off. His head rang with the powerful vibration and his eyes almost shook themselves loose from their sockets. The second chime actually knocked him off the ledge and he spiralled towards the ground.

The other birds stopped laughing and peered over the ledge, their initial sense of fun evaporating while they feared for Hatcher's safety. They needn't have worried. He righted himself and rejoined them, his wings clamping over his head when he touched down.

After all twelve bongs had echoed into the distance, Hatcher slumped against the clock-face. "How often does it do that?" he gasped.

Naz couldn't help himself. "Five times a day."

"Every two hours," Hatcher replied, nodding. "I thought so."

Ryker briefly forgot his troubles and almost fell off the tower himself. He eventually wiped away the tears of laughter and noticed that a jackdaw had alit on the far end of the ledge.

The bird strutted over confidently and introduced himself. "Hello, lads, I'm the Duke, and I seem to be missing out on all the fun."

"Duke of what?" Naz asked, noticing the other bird's mischievous white eyes, cocky gait and East End accent. He wasn't immediately sure if this bird could be trusted.

"Why, the Duke of Westminster, of course," the jackdaw replied. "You've landed on my patch and I thought I'd better check you out."

Ryker cast an eye over the large black bird with its distinctive silvery nape. "Do we pass your inspection?"

Duke appeared to subject him to intense scrutiny. "I haven't finished it yet but you look reasonably trustworthy. What brings you to town?"

"How do you know we're new here?" Naz asked.

"I can tell country birds a mile off because you were still standing on this ledge when the clock chimed," Duke replied with a smile. "The locals give Big Ben a wide berth on the hour."

Ryker decided to try his luck. "Do you know where the Feathered-Friends Park is?"

Duke snorted as if offended. "Pope Catholic, is he?"

"Ah, it's a test," Hatcher said eagerly, but his face dropped when he realised he didn't actually know the answer. "It's a tough one," he mumbled, scratching his chin with a wing and pacing up and down. After a while, and with the other birds staring open-mouthed, he shook his head. "It's going to have to be a guess, but I'll say he is."

"How did you work it out so quickly?" Naz asked, his voice laced with mock sarcastic incredulity. "The odds were only 50-50."

"I know!" Hatcher exclaimed. "What are the chances of that?" He puffed out his chest, delighted to have pleased everyone, and strutted off up the ledge muttering something about having a good education.

"How do you put up with him?" Duke asked.

"Lots of deep breaths," Naz replied quietly. "He's alright once you've bypassed the idiot."

Duke turned back to Ryker. "All got our problems, fella, haven't we? I'll point you in the right direction after you've given me a hand."

Hatcher held up both wings and searched himself. He was going to ask the obvious when Ryker waved him to silence.

"But we haven't got much time," Ryker said desperately. "My family is in trouble."

74

"The zoo could be anywhere then," Duke said evenly, waving a wing across the horizon. "Good luck." He could tell from the look on Ryker's face that the falcon wasn't used to negotiating solutions favourable to everyone. There was still a bit of youthful impatience about him. "Listen, my old china, ravens took my kids to the Tower of London. Something about shoring up the foundations in case it falls down. Only six of them left, see, and rumour has it when the last one leaves, the whole lot goes. But we jackdaws aren't strong enough to take them on. You help us free the kiddies and we'll return the favour."

Ryker looked to Naz for help and the owl nodded. He was older and wiser but wanted the falcon to learn about decision making and responsibility. He realised he'd led a sheltered life so it's what his parents would have wanted. He needed to acquire the spirit of co-operation too. Only then would he overcome his mental fragility.

"Ravens and us don't mix," Ryker said quietly. "And I'm not big on suicide missions."

Duke clapped him on the back. "Don't worry. I have a plan. Fly there, break in, rescue the littluns and escape," he explained. "Nothing to it really."

"Doesn't exactly smack of genius," Naz muttered.

"It's what I'd do," Hatcher said.

Duke walked to the ledge. "Come on. Follow me."

Naz was still sceptical but he followed the jackdaw into the air all the same. As Ryker drew alongside him, the owl said, "There'd better be more to it than that or we're going to get slaughtered."

Duke looked over his shoulder. "Is there."

The jackdaw dropped low over the river and headed downstream at a comfortable pace. He flew under several bridges before pulling up sharply and landing on Tower Bridge's upper walkway. The old stone prison opposite appeared grim and menacing. Ravens guarded each corner while two more circled above.

"That," Duke said casually, "was the easy bit."

Ryker landed next to him, gazed at the tower and shivered involuntarily. There was something evil about the place but he couldn't explain what it was. "How are you going to get in?"

"It's the getting out bit that worries me," Duke said. As he outlined his plan two more jackdaws dropped onto the walkway and strutted over. "Leave it to me and my brothers," he continued, not bothering with the introductions. "The ravens know we're here so we're going to need a distraction. While they're occupied with you lot, the three of us'll slip in through a storm drain on the riverbank. I've been using a file to weaken the bolts holding it in place every night for months. It leads directly into the tower, but it needs three of us to open. That's why you lot's a godsend because it frees us up to go to work. Anyway, I'll lead the kiddies out while Ryker takes out any raven that gets wise. Is that clear?"

"Crystal," Naz said. "Hawkins and I will lure them away, and Hatcher will confuse any raven that follows him."

"Ryker?" Duke said.

"I don't know how to take another bird down in flight," the falcon replied sullenly.

Duke took a step back. "Lived a pampered life, have we? It's high time you learned." The jackdaw stood in front of Ryker and lined his wing up with the falcon's beak. Then he turned and sighted on a statue across the river. "During the dive, keep the other bird lined up with the same point on the ground." Duke moved left and right and encouraged Ryker to keep him in front of the landmark. "Fastest bird in the world, aren't you, so you can't miss."

Ryker smiled as everything became clear. "I wish my father had explained it like that."

"I hate to interrupt the lesson," Naz said, "but those

ravens are starting to take interest."

Duke noticed the two lookouts circling above them. "Time to lead them on a wild goose chase downriver."

Hatcher pulled a face. "What's all this about geese?"

"Perhaps you'd be better off waiting here," Duke muttered.

"You can rely on me to do nothing particularly well," Hatcher said seriously. "I'm something of an expert."

Naz gave Hawkins a wink and they leaped off the bridge in formation. They circled the tower and the ravens took the bait, diving steeply to intercept them. Two more left their corner posts and joined the chase. Naz and Hawkins gave each other a knowing glance and hurtled across the river and under the bridge. They then accelerated east towards the sea. The ravens spread out in a diamond formation, cawing and hissing excitedly.

Duke gripped Ryker by the shoulders. "Fly cover above the tower. Either of those two ravens spots us, take 'em out."

Ryker nodded nervously. "You'd best get a move on in case the others come back."

Duke and his brothers dived towards the drain. They landed next to the pipe and put their combined weight against the grill covering the outlet. It finally squeaked open and they slipped inside.

Ryker jumped off the bridge and circled high above the tower to complete the distraction. The sentry ravens spotted him immediately and one took off to intercept him. Ryker remembered what Duke had taught him and rolled onto one side to begin his attack.

He lined the bird up with a streetlamp on the riverbank. No matter which way the raven jinked, Ryker kept it centred on the light. At the last moment, the raven realised it had been outmanoeuvred and tried to escape, but it was too late. Ryker made a tiny adjustment and flipped onto his left flank, extending his talons and knocking the smaller raven senseless with his first strike. It spiralled down and splashed into the river. Ryker inhaled deeply and clenched his talons. He'd done it!

He landed on the bridge, triumphant. The last raven knew it couldn't leave the tower and glared at him from a distance. Ryker brought his wing up and saluted. Then he saw Duke and a flock of smaller birds erupting from the drain. They spread out across the river to make their escape while his brothers brought up the rear. Duke led his two sons back up to the bridge and landed next to Ryker. Naz and Hawkins came hurtling in from the east at the same time.

"Those ravens haven't given up," Naz gasped.

Duke glanced over his shoulder. "Time to make like an egg!"

Hatcher shrugged. "Huh?"

"Beat it!"

They needed no coaxing and jumped off the bridge as one. With Duke leading, they took up an arrowhead formation and raced west towards the clock-tower and the safety of greater numbers.

Ryker took up a position at the tail of the flock. He heard one of the remaining ravens draw close, so he pulled up sharply and doubled back. He lined it up with an arch under one of the bridges and struck hard. The raven stood no chance, screeching and plunging into the river in its death throes.

Duke smiled when Ryker rejoined him. "And there you 'ave it."

"You make a pretty good teacher," Ryker replied.

"Jackdaw of all trades, ain't I," Duke said, his face turning serious again. "Only two of 'em left. Head for the eye."

Ryker frowned. "What do you mean?"

"The London Eye," Duke explained. "Lead them through the spokes. They haven't got the coordination to make it. They don't know that yet of course, which helps."

Ryker broke away from the formation and followed Duke towards the giant wheel on the far side of the river. The ravens ignored the flock and gave chase but one wisely refused to enter the maze of spokes. Ryker and Duke skilfully weaved in and out of the struts and the hasty raven immediately collided with the thick steel supports and crashed to the ground.

Duke couldn't suppress a broad grin. "Works every time! One to go."

Ryker glanced over his shoulder at the remaining raven. He was big and powerful with lifeless black eyes and a hooked beak. He didn't think he could fight him on his own. "How are we going to shake him off, Duke?"

Duke sized the raven up in a flash. "He's a big old brute so he'll tire quickly. Let's lead him a merry dance."

Ryker wasn't sure what the jackdaw meant but he eased into his slipstream and followed him this way and that around the skyscrapers. Every so often Duke would let the raven come within a few feet, and then he would suddenly pull up sharply to clear one of the buildings. Ryker suddenly understood what he was trying to do. The raven would close on them in the downward spirals but was using up valuable energy trying to keep on their tails in the climbs. After a while they could hear the raven gasping for breath as they circled the magnificent dome of St Paul's Cathedral.

Duke glanced at Ryker and nodded. "He's ready to go. Take a wing each on the next turn."

Ryker followed the jackdaw into a stomach-churning dive and then cut sharp right behind the Bank of England. The raven stooped to give chase and rounded the corner of the building but he was blowing hard and was almost spent.

Duke immediately doubled back. "Hit him hard,

Ryker!"

Ryker lined the big raven up and struck at his left wing. The raven was too exhausted to get out of their way and their combined assault stripped his wings of vital control feathers. The powerful raven screeched in surprise and found itself ploughing headlong into the building. Ryker and Duke looked on as it struck one of the columns and spiralled to the ground.

Duke ginned broadly. "The others will be worried. See you by the clock."

They landed on the Houses of Parliament a few minutes later. They were both tired and took a moment to catch their breath. The other birds crowded round and congratulated them.

Hatcher suddenly burst out laughing. "Brilliant!"

Naz frowned. "What's so funny?"

"Well, you of course. You're an owl, and this is Parliament." The pigeon clutched his sides and rolled about. "An owl. At Parliament. Hilarious!"

Duke was learning to ignore the pigeon, but he couldn't help himself. "Confused, is he?" He then clapped Ryker on the back. "See what we can do when we put our minds to it. Guess I owe you one." He pulled the falcon close and pointed his wing out west. "Take the river until it meets the motorway. Follow that for a couple of hours until you see the old stone monument."

"I'll recognise it from there," Naz said. "The zoo is just past the stones."

Duke nodded. "You'll be there by evening."

Ryker looked pleased that they were finally on their way. "Thanks, Duke."

"Don't mention it," the jackdaw said amiably.

Hatcher frowned. "Why ever not?"

Ryker checked the others were ready before leaping off the ledge. The warm afternoon air ruffled his feathers and a surge of adrenalin filled his veins as they headed into the unknown.

A small crack appeared at the base of the Tower of London. It spread half an inch, then stopped. A moment later a soft rumble shook the building, and the crack opened up a little more.

9

The birds left the city behind them. Every half hour they swapped positions to give the leader a rest and soon picked up the motorway heading west. Ryker couldn't help worrying about his family during their time on the wing. He became more determined than ever and pushed his friends hard, but the afternoon still dragged on.

Naz eventually guided them into a field next to the busy main road. "See the big brown sign with the cockatoo on it?" he said, panting with the exertion. "That means we're close. I suggest we grab something to eat and take a breather in the copse before making our move this evening."

There was a chorus of approval from the others, and they were soon relaxing in the shade of an elm tree on the edge of the field. If Ryker had had his way, they'd have over-flown the zoo now but Naz had warned him about the danger of being spotted by one of the keepers and reminded him to be patient.

As the sun fell behind the horizon, and the trees cast long shadows across the field, Naz looked at Ryker and nodded. "Now it's time. Are you ready?"

"You bet," he replied.

They'd spent some of the afternoon going over a plan, but Naz felt it prudent to give them a final briefing. "We'll land just inside the main entrance next to the Local Birds enclosure."

"That way we can blend in if we're spotted," Ryker added. He was beginning to come out of his shell and the other birds seemed to respect him immensely for it. "We'll try to find Cuthbert's friend first because if he knows what goes on here he could save us a lot of time."

"There won't be too many people on duty after hours," Naz said. "So we should be able to move around freely."

Ryker nodded. "Then we'll split into two groups of two to cover more ground."

"Why?" Hatcher asked. "Wouldn't it be easier for us to stick together in a group of four and have another group of nought? No one would spot a group of nought. It might as well be invisible."

"How would the group of nought tell us if it had found anything?" Naz asked seriously.

Hatcher nodded slowly, pensively. "We'd have to arrange to meet it somewhere at a certain time. Otherwise we might miss it altogether."

"Otherwise we might miss it," the other three birds said in unison, as if reading each other's minds.

For another brief moment Ryker forgot his troubles. He could barely remember anything so ridiculous, and the more he thought about the pigeon's suggestion, the more his sides ached. "Stop!" he gasped. "I can't take any more."

"I'll tell you what, Hatcher," Hawkins said, "why don't you lead the group of nought?"

"I hadn't thought of that," Hatcher said excitedly, puffing out his chest again. "There'd still be the three of you making up a group of four so we'd have an extra pair of eyes."

Naz's legs gave way and he rolled onto his back. "Brilliant. Brilliant."

"This is no laughing matter, Tony," Hatcher said eventually.

"Of course not," the owl replied. He sat up, took a deep breath and wiped the moisture from his eyes, then put on his best American accent. "Okay, team, let's saddle up and move out."

The others had just about recovered so they followed Naz into the field. The occasional set of car lights raced past in the night a hundred yards away, the motorway having quietened after the early evening rush. The owl stretched his wings. He was not quite ready to let Ryker take over as team leader because he still had a lot to learn, but Naz knew his strength of personality would one day stand him in good stead.

"I'm not going to give you a gung-ho pep talk," the owl said. "We've been through everything this afternoon so we all know what to do." Naz then leaped into the air knowing they were on his tail.

There was easily enough light from the moon to fly by. Hatcher went up next, circling once to make sure he was heading in the right direction. Ryker accelerated hard and soon caught them, while Hawkins was happy to bring up the rear.

It wasn't long before Naz pointed downwards. "There's the ancient stone monument."

Ryker followed his gaze. Lit up by different coloured floodlights were the Pillars of the Sun. The tourists had all gone home for the day and it was deathly quiet. The lighting cast eerie shadows around the site and he shivered. He wondered why the humans had built such a strange edifice.

The park was only a couple of minutes further and they were soon circling above it. There didn't appear to be much in the way of security so they dropped inside the tall perimeter fence and landed next to a number of large cages. The local birds eyed them up in silence. They were clearly in no mood to talk. Whether that was because they were wary of the intruders or worried about the consequences, Naz couldn't tell.

"Let's head up the path to the right," Ryker whispered.

The others followed and they regrouped on a bench by the parrot enclosure. The colourful birds also stared at them in silence.

"So far, so good," Naz said quietly, despite feeling that something wasn't quite right. "Hawkins, you fly with Hatcher from now on. We'll meet back here in half an hour."

They were about to go their separate ways when one of the parrots hopped over. "You're taking a big risk," she whispered.

Ryker stopped and turned. "I've got no choice. I'm looking for my family."

"It's dangerous to wander round the park at night," she replied. "Find them quickly and get out of here."

"Do you know if any falcons have been brought in recently?" he asked.

The parrot cocked her head as if thinking. "I remember some birds arriving in a truck a couple of nights ago, but it was dark and I couldn't see them properly."

"Do you know where they are now?" he asked.

She shrugged. "Some get taken to the lab on the far side of the zoo; others are put straight into cages."

Naz frowned. "What lab? I was here a couple of years back and I never saw a lab."

The parrot looked around nervously. "It's only just been finished. We're not treated as well now either."

"What do you mean?" Hawkins asked.

"Well the food's okay and the company interesting," she replied, "but the lack of freedom is a pain. It helps that we speak their language because it means we have a novelty value to them. Some of the older birds aren't so well looked after, however, especially now the lab's been built." She paused as if unsure about continuing.

Ryker sensed she was worried about her own safety. "Please, it might be important."

"It's only a rumour," she whispered, "but we think the lab might be used for conducting medical experiments. Much of what we hear is second hand but too many birds don't come out for my liking."

Ryker's heart sank. He could just imagine a scientist plunging an infected needle into Safiyya. He could hear her screams, imagine her fragile body convulse and lie still. "Is there a way in?"

"You need to speak to Seamus," the parrot said. "He's the golden eagle in the big enclosure up the path to your left. He's been here for as long as I can remember and knows everything that goes on in the park."

"Thanks for your help," he said. "I'm Ryker."

"Good luck, Ryker," she replied, declining to offer her name in case they were caught. "Keep an eye out for the guards. The lab struck a deal with the park's owners to provide security in return for having the lab inside the fence. They come round every half hour or so but they carry torches so you can spot them a mile off."

"Is that why most of the birds seem reluctant to talk?" Hawkins asked.

She nodded. "The guards get pretty nasty if they find out different species have been communicating. God knows why; it's not like we can coordinate an escape. Things were much better before the lab was built."

Ryker watched her hop back to her family. "Forgive the terrible pun but I say we shun good sense and put all of our eggs in one basket. Let's find Seamus."

Hatcher was about to tell them that despite his name he hadn't laid any eggs, but he thought better of it and followed them up the path. There were cages of all shapes and sizes. Some of the birds twittered noisy warnings while others took no notice of them whatsoever. Naz led the way as the path was enclosed by overhanging shrubs, interlocking vines and a couple of small trees, and light was low.

The eagle's cage was by far the largest they'd come across. This seemed pointless to Ryker as the bird still couldn't get the exercise it needed. High up on the far side he spotted a huge nest. It was a work of art: large twigs and small interwoven branches blended together to create an impressive structure. They could clearly make out the occupant, his eyes closed as if asleep. Ryker was about to try to get his attention when one of the eagle's eyes flicked open and fixed them with a curious stare.

"There's a guard coming," the eagle whispered in a soft Irish accent. "Hide."

The four birds looked around but could see no torchlight, no movement.

"Are you sure?" Ryker asked.

The eagle nodded. "You've got twenty seconds."

They looked around for somewhere to hide but there didn't appear to be any escape. A couple of torch beams briefly played across the cage and they froze. One guard was approaching from the main entrance and the parrot enclosure, while the other was coming from further up the path. They were trapped in the middle. Ryker desperately looked around but the trees and climbing plants were so thick they wouldn't have time to fight their way through. His heart felt like it would explode from his chest. Then he noticed Hawkins sizing up the gap between the cage bars. Being much smaller than the eagle they might just fit through!

"You can make it," the eagle said, "if you hurry."

They could hear the guards' footsteps now. Hawkins, Naz and Ryker slipped through sideways, but Hatcher was trying to get through head first and was wedged tightly between two bars. He wiggled his behind and squeezed through another inch.

The eagle stood and lifted his wing. "Jump in," he whispered. "I'll cover you."

Naz, Hawkins and Ryker leaped into the nest and crouched down low. But Hatcher was still stuck in the bars. Ryker was just about to get out and help him when a torch beam played over the far end of the cage.

"Get a move on!" he hissed.

Hatcher twisted his head and spotted the security guard no more than twenty paces away. With a final push he suddenly rocketed through the gap and hurtled into the bars opposite. Seamus caught a dazed Hatcher with his wing and dropped him into the bottom of the nest. The eagle then shielded them with his enormous brown wings, slowly easing his weight down until they were completely invisible.

Hatcher saw the size of the eagle's talons and gulped. They were as long as his body. He'd never felt so small. Even Ryker was dwarfed, he noticed. Ryker was also uneasy. Now he knew how the other birds had felt when they'd first met him.

The guards met in front of the cage and spoke briefly. They shone their torches into the enclosure but seemed satisfied that everything was normal. One pulled a cigarette from a packet in his top pocket and offered it to his partner. The second guard lit up and they chatted quietly for five minutes while they smoked. One stubbed his butt out on the bottom of his work boot and dropped it into a narrow drainage channel next to the cage. The other inhaled deeply, exhaled the bluish smoke into the night and flicked the butt at the eagle.

The burning ember landed on Seamus's back and singed his feathers. He knew he couldn't move or the others would be discovered so he had to endure the pain as it burned into his skin, causing a deep blister before it finally went out. The guards laughed at his discomfort. One then stopped and pointed at the cage. Seamus swallowed nervously, wondering what he'd seen. He closed his eyes and prayed, a bead of perspiration forming on his white brow feathers and rolling down onto his beak. He needn't have worried. The guard plucked one of Hatcher's feathers from the bars and showed it to his colleague. He examined it with a shrug and the two men went their separate ways.

As they disappeared down the path, Naz heard a jangling of keys. He peered over the rim of the nest, spotted a set hanging from the guard's belt and smiled.

The eagle exhaled slowly and allowed the birds out. "That was close," he said, his voice deep and resonant when he wasn't whispering. "Are you all okay?"

"Stone me," Hawkins said softly, "you're a big old so and so, aren't you? Thanks for that."

Seamus chuckled from deep within his generous belly. "You're welcome."

Ryker noticed the burn on his back and plucked the still warm embers from his feathers. "So much for the 'friends' part of the park's name," he said at last.

"They can be quite sadistic when the mood takes them," Seamus said calmly. He was clearly used to be being maltreated. "Don't worry; it'll heal in a couple of days."

"By which time we'll be long gone," Naz said.

"I didn't know they had golden eagles in Ireland," Hawkins said, changing the subject.

"Oh, I wasn't born there," Seamus replied. "I was raised in Scotland near Inverness, but my family was captured and sent to a zoo in the province when I was quite young. Over the years I lost the Scots accent and picked up the new one."

"How did you end up here?" Ryker asked. He was still shaking from their close encounter with the guards.

"The eagle they had died ten years ago," Seamus replied. "My family was brought in to replace him."

"Where are they then?" Naz asked.

There was a hint of sadness in the eagle's voice. "My chicks were shipped off to other zoos," he replied. "And my mate passed on a couple of months ago. They seem to be waiting for me to die before they bring in the next family."

"Well you're not going to die in here," Ryker said

firmly.

Seamus smiled. "If you help me escape, I'll do what I can for you."

Now it was Ryker's turn to smile. "I was hoping you'd say that. The parrot said the guards come round every half an hour so that gives us about twenty minutes to tell you our problem." He launched into their story, hoping that Seamus could shed some light on what went on in the lab on the far side of the park.

The eagle listened intently, nodding every so often as plans came and went, some promising, others discarded immediately. He waited patiently for Ryker to finish. "So you bumped into Cuthbert," he said, grinning at the mention of his old friend. "How's his leg?"

"Painful," Ryker replied, "which is all the more reason for you to help us."

Seamus bowed his head. "So he told you what happened."

Ryker nodded. "You grew up in the Highlands together. One day a hunter had you in his sights. Cuthbert distracted him so you could escape, and he took the hit instead. He told me only to bring it up if you didn't feel like helping us because he thought it might persuade you."

"You'd better count me in then," Seamus muttered with a wink.

"What can you tell us about the lab?" Ryker asked. Much as he'd have liked to talk to the eagle about his childhood, there was more immediate business to attend to. "Are my family being held there?"

Seamus could feel the desperation in Ryker's voice. "It's not part of the Feathered-Friends site," he began. "Helen the parrot was right. The place holds many a dark secret. We'll break in, find your family and make our escape before the guards know what's going on." He looked at the cage door and shrugged. "But all of this is meaningless unless you can get me out of here."

"That's where I come in," Naz said mysteriously. "But I'm going to need a diversion, which Ryker is going to provide."

10

Nigel drove through his local village and picked up the road heading out towards Leith Hill and its famous tower. It was a popular spot for tourists in the summer as the views across the South Downs were spectacular. By the time he arrived in the tower's deserted car park it was dark, however. Pine trees swayed in the breeze while lights from towns twinkled on the flat plains below. He pulled in and stopped underneath a tree on the far side. Then he waited. It was a familiar routine.

After about ten minutes another car pulled in, drew alongside the Mercedes and switched off its lights. Its window opened and a voice spoke quietly across the gap between the two vehicles. "Do you have the eggs?"

"The money hasn't cleared yet," Nigel replied. "By the time it does, they'll probably have hatched."

The gruff man nodded. "Fine. Bring them to me then."

"I'm expecting two more breeding pairs to arrive on Gordon's land by the end of the month," Nigel said.

The man in the other car nodded slowly. "Do they always nest on the cliffs?"

Nigel knew where the conversation was heading but he had to control himself. "Don't ask questions to which you already know the answer."

"Did he accept your offer?" the gruff man asked.

Nigel shook his head, the two men now visible to each other as their eyes became accustomed to the dark. "We're going to have to find another way to get rid of him. He seems to view our money as an inconvenience."

"You decide on the best way to do it and I'll make the necessary arrangements." The gruff man then changed the subject and passed across a piece of paper. "Here's a list of birds from my clients."

Nigel checked the sheet. "You could have emailed it."

"They can be traced," the mysterious man replied. "Let me know as soon as you have what they want." He reached into the back seat and handed Nigel a covered cage. "As you haven't caught the other falcon yet, you might need this. I'm sure the female will cooperate."

Nigel placed the cage on the passenger seat. "I'll call you tomorrow."

The gruff man wound his window up and eased his car onto the main road. Nigel pulled into his driveway ten minutes later and pressed a button on a remote control unit. His heavy entrance gates swung open quietly and he drove the half-mile up to the main house. He parked and carried the cage round to the farmyard. Chatter from the outbuildings died down immediately.

Nigel crossed the yard to a stable in the far corner and set the cage on the side. He approached another cage with a single female falcon inside. "I'd like you to meet your new mate," he said nastily. He picked up the covered cage, put it next to Safiyya and drew the cloth back.

A mangy old falcon shuffled forward, a lecherous gleam in his lifeless grey eyes. His pale feathers were falling out and he was covered in battle scars. He checked Safiyya from head to foot and smiled, a drop of saliva falling from his beak. Safiyya shuddered and backed up against her cage walls, her face a mask of terror and disgust.

Nigel pushed the cages together. "Don't worry," he sneered, "I'll let you get acquainted first." He laughed demonically and slipped next door.

There were two more caged falcons amongst rows of rare species crammed into the adjoining stable. They looked fit and healthy and defiant. Nigel undid a couple of catches that allowed the cage walls to slide in and out and turned a handle so they pinned the birds like a vice. They squawked noisily but were powerless against the pressure. They were soon held tight, their feathers pressing through the bars.

Nigel jabbed one of them in the flank with a needle from a cool box. It screeched in pain and gave him a nasty nip through the cage. The gamekeeper swore loudly. The bird's beak had removed a slice of skin from his thumb as neatly as a surgeon's scalpel. He washed the wound under a tap, rubbed in some antiseptic cream and wrapped a bandage round the entire thumb.

He walked back to the cage and stared at the birds. "You'll pay for that twofold," he whispered evilly, turning the cage screw one more revolution. "Enjoy your new home."

Nigel pressed the reset button on a digital clock on the wall and flicked the timer to stopwatch. He set it running, opened a diary on a small desk in the corner, and noted the time and his initial observations. "I'll be back to check on you in an hour," he said. "Don't go anywhere now." He laughed menacingly at his own joke and disappeared into the adjoining stable.

Algar and Mercia looked at one another in despair. They were held so tightly that it was almost impossible to move. Mercia coughed painfully and tried to shift to a more comfortable position but the cage bars dug into her middle. Her breathing was becoming erratic. A couple of feathers dropped to the cage floor.

"What do you think he injected me with?" she asked nervously.

Algar shrugged apathetically. "I don't know."

"We've got to get out of here and find Safiyya," she croaked.

Algar could feel the tension in his chest. "We can't do anything until the gamekeeper gets back."

Mercia noted the defeatist tone of his voice. "And where's Ryker? What's happened to our boy?"

Algar half turned and lowered his gaze to the floor. "He can't help us now, Mercia. He's probably already dead."

Mercia shook her head defiantly. "He's stronger than you think. You should have more faith in him."

"The last time I put my faith in him," Algar snapped, "we lost a daughter – him a sister."

She fixed him with a cold stare. "We've been through this. You shouldn't have left him alone with her. The difference is that I've forgiven you. Now it's your turn."

Algar wasn't going to back down. "If he'd learned his hunting skills, he could have killed that cuckoo. Instead it threw his sister out of the nest while he did nothing."

"You thought he was too young," Mercia replied angrily. "It's time you put this behind you. You've a son out there who needs his father. Besides, we have more immediate concerns, don't you think?"

This time Algar couldn't argue. The cage bit deeply into his flank. Blisters were forming on his skin. Time was not on their side.

Nigel opened the gate and started up the path through the woods with a feed bag thrown over one shoulder. Rory followed obediently at his heel. It was the dead of night but the moon offered just enough light to see by. He was about halfway along the path when the dog stopped again and growled. The gamekeeper huffed and tugged on his lead, the leather biting into Rory's neck.

"Come on, you mange-ridden mutt," he hissed. "This is no time to get the creeps."

He smacked the dog hard on its nose and took another couple of paces. Then he heard a noise up ahead. He strained his senses to try to make out what it was but the tree canopy was thick overhead and blotted out most of the moonlight. Nigel's heart quickened and beads of sweat formed on his brow despite the chill. His breath came in short pants as he inched forward, his eyes and ears peeled for the first sign of trouble.

He heard a rustling in the trees to his right and remembered the sheep's carcass. His heart thumped in his chest and blood roared in his ears. The sheep's remains were still in the tree but it was the animal feasting on it that rooted him to the spot. It was much bigger than the sheep, and jet black like a shadow. He could hear its powerful jaws crunching through bone and tearing flesh.

Nigel's mouth fell open and he dropped the bag. The creature turned at the noise and fixed him and the dog with a hypnotic stare, its huge yellow eyes trapping them like rabbits in the glare of a car's headlights. The gamekeeper finally came to his senses and ran, his jacket billowing out behind him, but his boots feeling like lead weights. Rory knew he was no match for the beast and also took flight.

The animal leaped to the ground behind them – its paws landing with only a soft patter – and gave chase. Nigel stumbled on in blind terror. He vaulted the gate in a single bound and charged across the yard without a backward glance. He threw open the front door and slammed it behind him, throwing a heavy bolt across to lock it. He staggered upstairs, grabbed a shotgun from a metal strongbox and collapsed onto the edge of his bed. He felt like he was going to have a heart attack. An almighty commotion then erupted in the yard. In the panic, he'd left Rory outside! The dog barked loudly, yelped once, and then there was silence.

Nigel poured himself a brandy and downed it, then poured another. He peered out of the window overlooking the yard but couldn't see anything. He drew the curtains and climbed back into bed, the floorboards creaking under his weight. He was still trembling as he finished off the second brandy but the alcohol was already calming his nerves. He turned off the light, rolled over and buried his head in the pillow as if it would erase what had just happened.

No sooner had he closed his eyes than the phone rang and he jumped. "What is it now?" he asked nervously.

"The world's top falconry event has been brought forward to next week," the gruff man replied. "My clients will pay a quarter of a million for your birds, but they need all four to secure the deal."

Nigel wiped his brow uneasily. "It's lucky I caught the other male then."

"You have him already?"

"Caged," Nigel lied.

"That was fast work," the man replied. "I'll collect them tomorrow. Don't be late."

Nigel hung up and fell into a light and troubled sleep.

11

Naz slipped through the cage bars and waited for Ryker to join him. "Are you ready?"

"Just say the word," Ryker replied confidently. "And stay right behind me."

"The word," Naz whispered.

Ryker took off quietly and headed up the path towards the lab. He knew Naz was on his tail because he could hear the longer, slower beat of his wings. They soon spotted the guard doing his rounds. He appeared bored and inattentive, the familiar routine dulling his senses. Ryker had every faith that the owl would get his bit right so he put his head down and concentrated on his fly by. He dropped low to the ground and followed the guard down the path next to the birds of paradise.

The guard suddenly heard their wing beats and turned but Ryker anticipated his reaction, whipped up in front of his face to confuse him and easily avoided his outstretched arm.

"Come here, you little blighter!" the guard shouted as he gave chase.

The distraction was complete.

Naz accelerated out of the shadows and swung his talons forward to pluck the guard's keys from his belt in one swift motion. He then doubled back and headed for the eagle's cage at top speed. He glanced over his shoulder to see Ryker leading the guard a merry dance down another path. Perfect.

When Naz reached Seamus's cage he held up the bunch triumphantly and slipped the largest key into the lock.

"Let's get you out of here," he whispered. He opened the cage and waved a wing in front of his chest as if acting the part of a royal courtier. "Please, I insist."

The birds slipped out and Naz locked the cage behind them. They headed up the path to the lab knowing that in the pre-dawn darkness no one was likely to spot Seamus was missing. When they reached the lab, they hid behind a kiosk offering visitors refreshments and guidebooks. There was a huge advertising hoarding next to the kiosk with a man's face on it.

Ryker crossed in front of it and dropped like a stone. "Looks like I've bought us a couple of minutes," he panted.

"Where's the guard?" Naz asked.

"Chasing shadows," Ryker replied. He nodded at the billboard. "What's that about?"

"He owns the park," Seamus replied. "He's the MP for agriculture and farming. He's supposed to be opening a new Birds of Prey enclosure next week."

"What's his name?" Naz asked.

"Craig Biggs," Seamus replied.

Naz studied the billboard. "I recognise him," he said eventually. "He used to come to Nigel's farm in the small hours to collect birds."

"There's a good chance some of them ended up here," Ryker said, turning their attention back to the lab. It was dimly lit and the tinted glass obscured what was going on inside. "Naz, you'd better go up now to keep watch."

The owl passed Hawkins the keys. "I'll tap on the windows if there's trouble." He was about to leap into the air when he spotted a guard approaching. "That's the guy who threw the cigarette butt at Seamus."

The eagle stiffened. "Payback time."

"What are you going to do?" Hawkins asked.

"I'm going to lay him out," Seamus replied casually.

The guard reached the lab steps and fumbled for his

keys.

"Go now!" Ryker hissed. "Before he realises his keys are missing and raises the alarm."

Seamus needed no coaxing. He took to the air and powered towards the lab entrance. The guard spun round at the last minute but he couldn't get out of the way. Seamus smashed into him at full tilt, the impact lifting the guard off his feet and pitching him forwards into the steps. He smacked his head on the concrete and lay still.

"Is he dead?" Hatcher asked. He hadn't spoken for a while, which they all thought was a blessing

"No," Hawkins replied. "Just out cold."

"What shall we do with his radio?" Ryker asked.

Seamus lifted the transmitter from the guard's belt and punched a hole in it with his beak. The plastic case split open and the interior wiring fell out. "Problem solved."

Ryker noticed a lump on the guard's forehead and a bruise spreading across his nose. "He'll only be out for about ten minutes so we'd best get inside."

Hawkins jumped onto the door handle and inserted the correct key in the lock. "Do come in," he said politely, mimicking the owl.

The modern, glass-enclosed foyer was low-lit and felt squeaky clean, but, apart from a brochure stand and drinks' dispenser, it was empty. Sets of double doors branched off from a white-washed central corridor behind the front desk.

"Do we take a room each or stick together?" Hatcher asked.

"We should stay together," Ryker replied. "If we come across anyone we'll confuse them with numbers."

"Clever," Hatcher muttered.

"Let's start on the left," Ryker continued, the tightness in his chest driving him on. His leadership skills were coming to the fore but he was clearly worried about what they might find. "We'll then work our way back to the main entrance to make our escape."

Seamus took the lead because he could reach all the door handles. The first was unlocked and opened into a dark chamber of indeterminate size. Hawkins leaped up and flicked the light switch and they blinked on one by one. The birds entered the room and stopped. It was crammed from floor to ceiling with hundreds of cages. Most of the captive birds were quiet but some murmured in hushed tones when they spotted the odd-looking group in the doorway.

Ryker's hopes lifted. There was a chance his family were being held here. He flew up and down the rows but his hopes soon receded. There was no sign of them. Tears welled in his eyes. He took one last look round the chamber and joined the others in the hall.

Seamus opened the next door and a blast of cold air billowed into the corridor. Ryker entered the freezer. It was probably no more than ten feet wide but rows of shelves on either side held all sorts of medical equipment and tissue samples. Each one was carefully labelled, but the birds couldn't understand anything. The blood samples were an ominous sign though. Things were getting dangerous, but there was nothing more they could do here so they pushed on.

Seamus opened the door opposite, which led into an office. There was a coffee table next to a large leather sofa under the window; two bookcases stretching from floor to ceiling; and a huge ornate wooden desk.

Hatcher hopped onto the desk and promptly tripped over the computer keyboard. The monitor came to life and the base station whirred. "Ooops," he said as a disc popped out of the drive. "I think I've just broken something. Who wants to play Frisbee?"

"This is no time for fun and games," Hawkins said exasperatedly. "But seeing as you found it, we'd better take it. Can you see a box for it?"

Hatcher marched to the end of the desk and passed the case to the kestrel.

Hawkins removed the disc and popped it inside. "Exhibit A," he announced, dropping it into a bag he'd found in a bin under the desk.

"We're done here," Seamus said. "Let's move on."

Ryker slipped out first. There was only one more room to check. Seamus patted him on the back and opened the last door. It was a good thing they'd been quiet because there were two technicians on the far side of a vast laboratory. They had their backs to the door and appeared to be administering something to a bird in a glass cage with a large syringe.

The birds crept inside, their mouths dropping. This was clearly the nerve centre of the operation. It was similarly laid out to the holding chamber opposite but the majority of the work clearly went on here. Birds were being tested for all sorts of diseases, deliberately infected with others, and used for a multitude of cosmetic tests. Their suffering was evident.

One of the technicians suddenly stood upright and the birds froze. They needn't have worried because he simply started a stopwatch. He nodded to his partner and they both disappeared through another door in the far wall. The birds were alone, if only for a few moments.

Ryker needed no invitation. He leaped into the air and flew directly to the glass case. A falcon was lying on its side twitching. "Safi!" he gasped.

The falcon rolled over, her face contorted with pain. "Lizzie," she coughed. "Who are you?"

Ryker's heart fell through the floor. "I'm sorry," he said, his mind whirling. "I thought you were somebody else."

The other birds joined Ryker at the case.

"It's not her," he mumbled.

"Please get me out of here," she whispered.

"What was the injection for?" was all he could think of saying.

She shuddered at the thought of the needle piercing her flesh. "They're trying to stimulate egg production so that the falcons in the park can father more chicks. The birds here are just used as guinea pigs."

"Don't be ridiculous," Hatcher said. "You haven't got a snout. Or trotters."

"Have they forced you to mate?" Ryker asked, ignoring the pigeon.

The falcon shook her head. "Not yet. But if they can't find a suitable male, they'll use one of the older falcons instead. I can't bear the thought of it."

Ryker's face fell again. There were hundreds of questions running through his mind but they'd have to wait. "I promise you this place will soon be shut down. Hang in there."

The falcon looked him in the eyes and shook her head. "Don't leave me!"

"There's nothing we can do now," Ryker replied forlornly. "You're going to have to trust me."

They were interrupted by a tapping on the window.

"That'll be Naz," Hawkins said. "We have to leave now."

The birds were halfway back to the door when the scientists returned. They immediately spotted the flock and charged across the room waving their arms and shouting.

Ryker dived into the corridor and waited for the eagle by the main entrance. "There's a light coming up the path," he whispered, the urgency of the situation not fazing him. He was thinking clearly under pressure now, a new sense of purpose filling him. "We'd better make a break for it."

The eagle pushed the door open and the birds flitted past the guard into the night. "After you."

Naz landed by the steps. "This bloke is coming round and there's another on the way!"

"Naz, you lead," Ryker said. "Hatcher and Hawkins will follow, while Seamus and I bring up the rear. Go! Time's flying!"

The scientists burst through the lab doors and charged across the atrium gesturing wildly.

Ryker waited for Seamus and then followed the others into the air. They weren't a moment too soon. Seamus had only just cleared the building when the scientists crashed through the front doors and found the guard lying on the ground outside. The second guard saw what was happening and raised the alarm, the lab building and surrounding park lighting up like a Christmas tree.

Ryker stole a glance behind him. Its secret out at last, the laboratory's lights faded into the night like a bad dream. He checked they were all in formation before drawing alongside Naz and telling him Lizzie's story. "Is that how Nigel produces eggs on his farm, Naz? Does he mate lone females with falcons from the zoo?"

Naz turned away. "I'm not sure."

Ryker suddenly understood. "Naz, tell me the truth! Without me, Nigel is a male short."

The owl nodded slowly. "I didn't want to worry you."

Tears were forming in Ryker's eyes as the realisation dawned on him that Safiyya might have been paired with another falcon. His heart felt like it was being squeezed between two blocks of ice. "You should have told me," he whimpered.

"We don't even know if she survived the fight," Naz countered. "And what good would it have done to tell you? You'd only have gone back to Nigel's and got yourself caught. Then we'd never have made it here to free Seamus. Now we know we can fight back."

"I hope we're not too late," Ryker said desperately.

12

The gamekeeper woke early the next morning. He was still tired and shivered involuntarily. It was cold in the bedroom and condensation was gathering on the windowsills. Some of the paint was peeling away and the wood was rotten in places. Nigel was still dressed so he swung his legs out of bed, cradled the shotgun under one arm and went downstairs.

He slowly opened the front door and peered across the yard. It was quiet. Rory was nowhere to be seen. He walked over to one of the stables and moved some boxes aside until he found what he was looking for. He smiled, exposing an uneven set of stained teeth, and whispered to himself, "This should even things up a bit."

He carried the heavy steel trap into the yard to check it over. Its teeth were razor sharp and stained with the blood of countless animals. He brushed a few cobwebs away from the spring and made sure it was working. Then he slung the shotgun across his back and carried the trap into the woods.

The morning sun bathed the path and he had no trouble finding the tree. He approached cautiously to avoid startling the beast for a second time but the woods were deathly quiet. He attached the trap to the base of the tree and pried the jaws apart with a lever. Then he covered the steel teeth with loose twigs and leaves. He stepped back and admired his handiwork. The trap was all but invisible.

The sheep's remains were still wedged in the crook so the beast would definitely be back. Half the carcass had been devoured the night before leaving only the hindquarters. Nigel shuddered and checked that both shotgun barrels were loaded. He felt for some spare cartridges in another pocket just in case. Then he collected the bag of feed and headed for the field. Except for Dillon and Flint, who were waiting on fenceposts, the ravens and cuckoos scattered at his approach. The magpie watched from a distance because she didn't want the gamekeeper to know too much about her.

Nigel leaned the shotgun against the fence and tipped the bag's contents into a trough. "I need the other falcon by tonight," he said eventually. He waved a hand across Gordon's field. "Bring him to me and all this will be yours." He then shouldered the shotgun again and marched off down the path.

Flint looked at Dillon. "Well?"

"Simple," Dillon said. "We'll hit the Redlands birds while they're least expecting it and lure the falcon back here on a revenge mission. We'll let him get as far as Nigel's yard where he'll fly straight into a trap. Tell Jolenta the plan and meet me here at midday."

Nigel checked the trap on his way past. It was perfectly camouflaged. He couldn't help wondering what had happened to Rory so he searched the clearing. He was about to give up when he spotted a small metallic object glinting in the sunlight. It was Rory's nametag. Nigel picked it up and wiped away the blood. He scanned the bushes once more, gun at the ready, but there was no sign of the dog so he headed back to the yard.

He opened the stable door and checked on Algar and Mercia. Having been clamped fast by the steel bars overnight they were in considerable pain. Some of their feathers were falling out, their eyes were bloodshot and they had sores on their bodies. Nigel smiled and went

106

next door to check on Safiyya. The mangy old falcon still had his eyes on her but she had managed to fall asleep.

Nigel shook the cage and woke her. "Can't have you napping on the job."

The gamekeeper crossed back to the main house, his feet squelching in the muck, and entered his study. He switched on his computer and scrolled through a list of birds he had in his barns. He was in the middle of cross-checking it with the list given to him the night before when the phone rang.

"One of my birds has escaped from the zoo," the gruff voice said.

"Which one?" Nigel asked.

"The eagle."

Nigel swore softly to himself. "How? The place is supposed to be secure."

"He had help."

"Did someone break in?" Nigel asked.

"Something rather than someone," the gruff man replied. "My staff are giving statements now but CCTV picked up an owl, a pigeon, a kestrel and," he paused for effect, "a peregrine falcon. What are the chances of that?"

Nigel took a deep breath. "That can't be."

"You lied to me, Nigel," the gruff man said angrily. "You told me you'd captured it!"

"How do you know it's the same falcon?" Nigel asked, desperately searching for a way out.

"Because the owl helping him is the one that escaped from your farm," the man replied. "He's got that unusual white tuft on his chest. Two and two always equals four, and maths is my strong suit."

"Your people are incompetent," Nigel hissed, trying to turn the tables and blame the loss on his partner's security team.

"Tread carefully, Nigel," the man spat. "I can close you

down with a single phone call."

"Shut my farm and you go down too," Nigel replied evenly. "Then you'll never see that falcon. That won't please your clients – they strike me as the sort of people who don't take bad news very well – so you'll be constantly looking over your shoulder."

"Is that a threat?"

"No," Nigel said flatly. He was finding it hard not to lose his temper. His arrangement with the other man was purely business. On a personal level they despised each other. "We must work together to put Gordon out of business and claim his land so I'm simply reminding you of the facts. If one of us takes a fall, the other joins him."

"One thing is for sure," the voice said. "That'll never happen to me."

Nigel bit his tongue, took a deep breath and stepped back from the edge. "What do you want me to do?"

"The falcon will follow its homing instinct and head back to Redlands," the gruff man said. See to it that there's a reception committee. Lie to me again, however, and I'll put you out of business. Permanently."

13

Gordon woke later than usual. He sat up in bed and stretched, then pulled on a dressing gown and went downstairs to make a cup of tea. He stirred in a couple of sugars and collected the weekend paper from the doormat. He'd only just sat down at the kitchen table when he heard a gunshot in the distance. He looked up but thought nothing of it. It was a common sound in the countryside. A couple of minutes later he heard one of his dogs whimpering in the yard.

He opened the back door and almost dropped his tea. The dog had been shot and was bleeding from wounds in its rump. He knelt to examine him and shook his head angrily. "Oh, Buster," he said quietly. "That does it, Nigel!"

Gordon carried Buster to the car and placed him gently in the boot. He covered him with a blanket and ran back into the house to get dressed. He grabbed his car keys from the hook by the front door and crossed the yard to put the other animals away. If someone was prepared to shoot a dog, who knows what else they might do.

He called the other dog in from the garden and put him in the back seat, then drove up to the animal sanctuary. When he pulled into the car park he noticed Nigel's Mercedes was already there. He shook his head, barely able to contain his anger, and carried Buster to the main entrance. He marched past a startled receptionist into the treatment room, his face like thunder. Simone was attending to yet another pheasant while Nigel had his back to him.

Gordon slammed the door. "What's the meaning of this?"

Nigel casually half-turned, but refused to meet Gordon's eyes. "The meaning of what?"

Simone took one look at Buster and frowned. "Good Lord, he's been shot. Lay him on the recovery table."

Gordon carefully placed Buster on the work surface and refaced the gamekeeper. "You know exactly what I'm talking about, Nigel."

Nigel shook his head but there was no disguising the evil glint in his eyes. "No, I don't. Now please excuse us. Simone and I have matters to discuss."

Gordon rubbed Buster's ears. "What matters?"

"Our dinner date, if you must know," Nigel replied, turning his back on Gordon. "It's a private conversation."

Gordon looked at Simone, his face falling. "Tell me you're not seeing him."

The vet finished bandaging the pheasant's leg. "Gordon, please!" she begged. "You're not helping."

"Yes, Gordon," Nigel smirked.

The farmer pointed a finger at the gamekeeper. "When did he arrive, Simone?"

She shrugged and checked the clock on the wall. "About ten minutes ago. Why?"

"Is that all," Gordon spat.

Simone stood up straight and put her hands on her hips. "I don't know what the problem is between you two," she began, "but you can take it elsewhere. I must tend to Buster. You can both wait outside."

Nigel let the door close behind him instead of holding it open for Gordon. The two men faced each other in the hallway, the friction between them about to create fire.

Gordon inched closer. "I suggest you leave now."

Nigel chuckled. "Are you going to make me?"

Gordon stood up straight and puffed out his chest. He

was still several inches shorter than the gamekeeper but he was far more powerfully built. "If I have to."

They stared at each other for an uncomfortably long time before Nigel wisely backed down. "You haven't heard the last of this," he said quietly.

"You may be able to pull the wool over her eyes," Gordon countered, "but you don't fool me. No wonder your wife and friends deserted you."

Nigel smiled evilly and leaned closer, his stale breath smelling of cigarettes. "But I'm going out for dinner with Simone. Where does that leave you, Gordon? Home alone?" He winked, then turned and left the building.

Gordon stared after him and clenched his fists but he eventually calmed down and re-entered the treatment room. He stroked Buster and opened his mouth to say something.

Simone cut him off. "I don't want to talk about it."

Gordon looked at the floor. "Is he going to be okay?" he asked softly.

Simone nodded, but spoke as if lecturing someone she didn't know. "Some shot passed through the flesh on his hindquarters but I've managed to dig it all out. I'll clean and dress the wound and he should be right as rain in a few days."

Gordon rubbed his chin as if unsure how to broach the subject but ended up coming straight out with it. "Nigel was behind this."

Simone's eyes made her position clear. "Don't be ridiculous, Gordon. I don't know why you've got it in for him. Perhaps you're jealous. Whatever it is, I don't like it." She gripped his arm. "Now, please wait outside until I'm finished."

Gordon had no option but to wait in reception. He picked up one of the magazines but didn't see the words so he gave up and stared out of the window.

Simone carried Buster out of the treatment room a few

minutes later and they walked into the car park. "Make sure he gets a couple of days' rest."

Gordon opened the boot and carefully placed him inside. He was about to reason with Simone when a large shadow passed overhead. The farmer leaned back and shielded his eyes against the sun. "Now there's something you don't see every day."

Simone followed his gaze. "Certainly not round here. Golden eagles are extremely rare."

14

Ryker led the birds across the fields on the outskirts of Boxhill. They'd been in the air for several hours and were beginning to tire, but still he drove them on. The town centre was bustling with shoppers perusing the world-famous antique shops. And the townsfolk were gearing up for the festival – which had taken the place of more traditional Mayday events – in aid of the local vineyard, whose vines had suffered frost damage the year before. As the wines were the main contributor to the local economy, the locals were gathering in force to taste the previous year's vintage. They were also hoping to catch a glimpse of the cycle race and several shop owners had already marked out their stalls on the pavement.

And then they were leaving the town behind, its emblem, a huge silver cockerel overlooking the park, fading into the distance. Ryker pushed them hard into the home stretch. They passed a small hamlet before spotting Gordon's farm. There were no birds in the sky above Redlands. Ryker led them to the stream and landed in the field. He was exhausted, long hours in the air and the effort of the previous night taking its toll. He took deep breaths to calm his racing heart and waited for the others to join him.

Seamus came in next. He hadn't been able to stretch his wings for years and he was dead tired. Naz was as fit as a fiddle, so too Hawkins. They probably could have gone on indefinitely.

"Lucky I know where I live," the pigeon said presently, "otherwise we could have got lost on the way back."

"Thank God for small mercies," Naz muttered.

"We should find Cuthbert," Ryker said, setting off into the woods. "With any luck he and Wilbur will have refined the plan for liberating Nigel's farm."

It was quiet in the forest, and it soon became clear why. Every few paces they came across the body of a bird lying twitching in the leaves. Ryker stopped and examined a young female blackbird, then a juvenile blue-tit and then a thrush chick. They all looked the same, their eyes almost lifeless, their bodies mutilated by the savage ravens. The nests above them were also quiet. Ryker could barely contain his anger.

They reached the clearing a few minutes later. Ryker spotted a pheasant lying on its side against the tree trunk and his heart skipped a beat. It was Wilbur and he was in a bad way. His eyes were puffy and red and there were scratches on his body. Ryker touched him lightly on the shoulder.

Wilbur stirred and tried to get to his feet. "Thank the Lord, you're back," he whispered. There were little flecks of discoloured spittle around his beak. "My brother will be here in a minute. Pull up a chair." Despite his condition Wilbur maintained his dignity and sense of humour. He coughed a couple of times but his breathing was laboured. "They came this morning."

Ryker helped him up. "How bad is it?"

Wilbur steadied himself. "None of us escaped. You're too late."

"It's never too late," Ryker said, the anger rising inside him once again. "Where is Cuthbert?"

"Collecting food," Wilbur replied. "He knew you'd need to get your strength up."

Almost before he'd finished his sentence, Cuthbert appeared by the fallen tree. He'd been worked over but his eyes brightened when he saw them and he smiled thinly through the pain. "Seamus, mon ami," he said, embracing

114

his old friend, "how the devil are you?"

Seamus was clearly upset at what had happened but he managed to return his smile. "I wish our reunion had a happier setting."

Cuthbert nodded, a look of determination on his face. "We'll have to show some Highland fighting spirit in the coming battle and have a huge party afterwards." His enthusiasm and confidence were infectious and their mood improved. He then turned to Ryker and gave the falcon a fatherly squeeze. "Did you find your family?"

"They weren't at the zoo," Ryker replied, "so they must still be at Nigel's. And we found out what really goes on at Feathered-Friends." He told the pheasants their story and held up the bag with the computer disc. "I'd better take this to Gordon because he'll know what to do with it. When I get back we're going to take down those ravens."

"Patience," Cuthbert said. "That's exactly what they want us to do and I'll not play into their talons. While you were gone I amended my plan to liberate the gamekeeper's farm. We finally have the personnel to make it work, but we must agree on the strategy. I'll brief everyone while you're at Gordon's, but you can expect to go tonight."

As the situation reached crisis point Ryker was getting more involved. He was becoming a focal point for the group, but Cuthbert knew he still had to learn to weigh all the options first. In turn Ryker drew strength from them, knowing that they'd back him when the time for action came. He headed into the woods and soon reached the edge of the field. He leaped into the air, feeling a surge of anticipation as he swept across it.

Gordon's farm also seemed unusually quiet. There were no animals in the yard and no livestock in the fields. Ryker's initial confidence began to evaporate. He stooped into a dive and came in fast. There was no Eadric to greet him and no grain in the feed troughs. He was about to carry the bag over to the farmhouse when the cockerel poked his head round the door to one of the henhouses. Ryker could tell he was flustered because his face was red and he was perspiring.

"Well, if it isn't the shy rooster," he said.

Eadric looked a little embarrassed. "I was just seeing what all the fuss is about."

Ryker laughed. "About time."

The cockerel shuddered. "I'm not sure it's all it's cracked up to be."

"Well at least you gave it a shot," Ryker said with a sigh. He wondered how the cockerel would react to the menace that faced them, particularly when he found out there might be an altercation with the Ravenswood birds, so he played down the threat considerably. "Listen, Eadric, the ravens attacked Redlands this morning."

The cockerel nodded. "That's why Gordon put all the animals away."

"We need all the help we can get," Ryker explained, "because we're going to fight back."

Eadric gulped and shrank back into the henhouse. "I'm not comfortable with physical confrontation, Ryker."

It wasn't all he wasn't comfortable with, Ryker thought. "The more birds we can muster, the greater our show of force. It might put the cuckoos off coming onto Gordon's land."

"To be honest," Eadric muttered, "I'd rather get back to the hens."

"I think we both know that's not true," Ryker replied.

Eadric didn't look happy but eventually he gave in. "I can't stay airborne for long."

"You can be our eyes on the ground then," Ryker said.

Eadric looked as if he might start strutting around the yard. "I like the sound of that."

"I need to give this to Gordon first," Ryker said, holding up the bag with the disc.

116

"I think he's out," Eadric replied. "He took Buster up to the sanctuary because he'd been shot. Leave it on the back porch."

Ryker guessed the shooting might have something to do with Nigel, but he didn't want to worry Eadric any more than necessary. He dropped the bag in a log basket and rejoined the cockerel in the yard. "Okay, let's do it," he said, taking to the air and hoping that by the time they got back Cuthbert's plans had been finalised.

As they crossed the field, Ryker stole a glance at the distant cliffs. He hadn't the courage to fly past the nests on the way to Gordon's but an inner sense told him to stop by on his return. "I need to check on something, Eadric," he said. "I'll meet you down by the stream in a minute."

Eadric peeled away and Ryker approached the steep white walls for the first time in what seemed like ages. There were no signs that his family had been back to the nests, which were still scattered across the ledge. He couldn't explain why he'd been drawn back so he wrote it off as homesickness. He was about to rejoin the cockerel when he heard a screech of pain from Ravenswood. It reminded him of the noise the fox made when he'd fought with it in Gordon's yard.

He looked across the field to the stream and then back at Ravenswood. He was caught in two minds. Eadric and the others would be waiting for him, but there was a chance the fox was in trouble. He went against his better judgement and swooped down towards the estate. He landed on a branch and checked the raven nests above him. They were all quiet. With a deep sense of foreboding and real fear rising in his stomach, he dropped to the ground and tiptoed along the path into the woods. It hadn't escaped him that he was going against his father's wishes yet again.

He soon heard a commotion up ahead and approached cautiously. Then he peered into a clearing from behind a tree stump. The fox had been snared by Nigel's trap. She was trying to free herself from its vicious teeth but was only drawing blood from a deep gouge in her tail. Ryker took another cursory glance around and trotted into the clearing.

"Need a hand?" he asked quietly.

The fox stopped and shook her head. "I told you before, I work alone."

Ryker shrugged and turned to leave. "Don't say I didn't ask."

The fox watched him go, her face finally registering the seriousness of the situation. She swallowed her pride and coughed. "Wait! What was it you said about co-operation?"

Ryker stopped. "We can only beat Nigel and his ravens if we work together."

The fox nodded slowly. "Will you help me?"

Ryker read the distress in her voice, the pain of what she was asking. He was so engrossed that he didn't notice a cuckoo landing on a branch far above. It was joined by a raven, then another, and another. He smiled and wandered across the clearing towards the fox. "If it makes us allies."

"I don't think I have a choice," she replied.

Ryker nodded at the sheep's carcass above the trap and shuddered. "Did you kill it?"

The fox shook her head. "I could never have dragged it into a tree. I'm so hungry I've been reduced to scavenging."

"Then what did?" Ryker asked, breaking off a short branch and wedging it between the trap's jaws.

"Something a lot bigger and stronger than me," she replied mysteriously.

Ryker couldn't imagine such an animal so he concentrated on springing the trap. He knew Eadric would be waiting by the stream but the cockerel would have to put up with the delay. "When I lever it open, pull yourself

118

free."

He carefully positioned the branch next to the spring and jumped on the free end. The trap popped open for a fraction of a second and the fox whipped her tail out. She wasn't quite quick enough, however, and the trap severed the last six inches. She hissed in pain and licked her wounds.

"Thanks, Ryker," she said eventually.

He raised the feathers above one eye. "How do you know my name?"

"Everyone knows you're trying to find your family," she replied. "I'm Lufu."

"I hope we can be friends," Ryker said.

"It's not in my nature to trust anyone else," she said slowly, "but in your case I'll try to make an exception."

Ryker was about to reply when he noticed a small movement in the trees out of the corner of his eye. He could have sworn a cuckoo just slipped behind a branch.

"What's wrong?" Lufu asked.

"Time to trust me," Ryker shouted. "Run!"

Lufu didn't have time to question him. The ravens burst from the trees and swooped down on them but Ryker had given them just enough of a head-start and they bolted for the field. Lufu had dug her way under the fence by the hide and she dived into the hole. She reappeared a moment later and slipped into the long grass. Ryker expertly weaved in and out of the trees and raced across the field above her. He caught the fox's eye and winked as they went their separate ways in case any ravens followed.

Dillon pulled his flock up short and held out his wing. "Let them go. We'll get our chance later. When we do, leave the kill to me. Everyone should know why these woods bear my name!"

Ryker darted across to Redlands and landed next to Eadric.

"Come with me," he said, following the stream into the woods. "Sorry I took so long."

Eadric didn't ask what had kept him and the falcon didn't offer an explanation. There would be time for that later. The other birds were on a war footing and almost snapped into action at their approach.

"It's only me," Ryker said. "I've brought a friend."

"The more the merrier," Cuthbert said. "I've just finished outlining the plan."

"Is there anything I need to know?" Ryker asked.

Cuthbert nodded. "We must release your family first so they can join us in the fight. Seamus will draw the ravens out and we'll make our move while they're distracted."

Ryker clenched his talons in anticipation of a personal battle with Dillon. "When do we go?"

Cuthbert glanced at the setting sun. "Now."

Nigel left the supermarket car park and turned onto the main road. Things were falling into place nicely. It wouldn't be long before Gordon would be forced to accept an offer on his farm. All he needed now was the other falcon.

He glanced towards the cliffs as a shadow passed in front of them. He screeched to a halt at the side of the road and grabbed a pair of binoculars from the passenger seat. He adjusted the focus, his jaw dropping when he identified the magnificent eagle. "Sorry, Mr Biggs," he whispered, "but that's one for the trophy cabinet."

He pulled into his driveway and parked by the front door. He jogged inside and unlocked a cabinet in the hallway. Then he pulled out a tranquilliser gun and checked it was loaded. He dropped a couple more darts into his pocket, pulled on a hunting jacket to ward off the early evening chill and collected the shotgun. He then crossed the yard to where Flint and Dillon were waiting on the gatepost.

"They think they can use an eagle to draw us out," he

said quietly. "With no one guarding the barns, they'll try to sneak in to rescue the other falcons. Send your weakest birds into battle first because they're expendable. Have them lure the eagle towards me." He patted the gun's stock. "Their morale will collapse if I take him down first. Organise a reception committee in case any get through."

A gleam appeared in Dillon's charcoal black eyes. He leaped off the fence and led Flint towards the field. "You heard the man," he said. "Bring your flock to me."

Nigel screwed a torch to the tranquilliser gun's telescopic sights and followed them into the woods. The light was fading fast. He noticed that the trap had been sprung but nothing had been caught in its jaws. He searched the undergrowth in case the animal had escaped and was dying in the bushes but all he could find was the remains of the tail. "That was no fox," he muttered.

Nigel eventually crawled into the hide. He pulled a branch across the entrance and took careful aim at the cliffs. The eagle practically filled his scope. He checked the raven nests above him to make sure they were massing for the attack. Then he flicked the torch on and off so Dillon would know he was ready.

Gordon pulled up to Pond Farm and switched off the car engine. He suddenly felt extremely tired. He climbed out and glanced at the cliffs, realising immediately that something wasn't right. A vast cloud of ravens burst from the woods and quickly surrounded the eagle.

Gordon banged his fist on the car bonnet. "Not again!"

He ran inside and collected his shotgun from a strongbox in the lounge. He checked it was loaded and trotted down to the field.

The Battle of Boxhill had begun.

15

Ryker gazed up at the cliffs from under an oak tree by the stream. Seamus was fighting off the ravens with great skill and courage and he repeatedly knocked them to the ground.

Cuthbert drew them in close. "Our distraction is working. We must go now to sneak in under their radar. Wilbur is too badly injured so he'll look after the nests here."

"Okay," Ryker said. "Let's go!"

He leaped into the air and flew low across the field towards the rising moon, his heart racing at the coming confrontation. Ravenswood had its customary menace, all dark and forbidding, but Ryker made it across the field unchallenged. He checked over his shoulder and noticed Hawkins, Naz, Hatcher and Cuthbert had fanned out behind him in a tight formation. He swooped into the trees and skilfully avoided the low branches but he daren't set down until he reached Nigel's yard. He eventually landed on the roof of one of the barns and shivered. It was quiet, too quiet.

The gamekeeper watched them from the hide, then gave Dillon another signal before taking careful aim at the cliffs. It was time to wrap this up before it had started.

Ryker nodded at one of the barns. "My dad was in that one," he whispered. "But I need to find Safi and our eggs

122

first."

"We should split up," Hawkins said. "I'll help Cuthbert release your dad. Naz and Eadric can go with you."

"That leaves me as the lookout," Hatcher said proudly. "You're in luck." He'd hardly finished his sentence when the moon disappeared behind a cloud and he tripped over a loose roof tile and banged his beak on the wall.

They all froze but the yard was quiet. No lights came on, no dog barked.

"We'll meet back here shortly," Ryker said. "Then we'll release all the other birds before heading back to Redlands to help Seamus."

Hawkins and Cuthbert swooped across the yard to look for Ryker's parents, while Naz and Ryker tried one of the other barns. They landed on a windowsill and glanced inside. There were rows of cages holding all kinds of rare species. The window was ajar.

Ryker looked at Naz and shrugged. "I guess we're going in."

"I'll wait here," Eadric said.

Something nagged at the back of Naz's mind but he couldn't work out what it was. "After you, bro'," he said, holding out a wing to Ryker. He followed the falcon inside, but didn't notice a catch on the window. "You take the first row."

Ryker dropped to the floor and began checking hundreds of cages. There was a familiar smell mixed in with all the other birds' scents. It was unmistakeable. Safiyya was here! He passed Naz, shrugged and started on the next aisle.

Suddenly Safiyya called out from a cage in the far corner. "Ryker, get out! It's a trap!"

Ryker leaped into the air and raced towards her. "Safi!"

He'd only made it about halfway across the barn when ravens burst in through every window and door. Ryker sliced through the first wave and swung round to find Naz. The owl was barrelling towards him, a group of five ravens slashing at his tail.

"Go for the window we came in!" Naz bellowed.

Ryker lashed out at another raven, distraught that Safi would have to wait, but if they were caught now it was all over. He raced down the aisle with Naz in hot pursuit. The window was still open. He brushed past another two ravens and put his head down. They were only a few feet from the window when his heart sank. Eadric was being escorted away by two ravens while more looked on with beaks bared. One of them kicked the window shut and locked them in. Ryker and Naz turned to face the angry flock but they were hopelessly outnumbered.

Their rescue attempt had failed.

"Bring them to me," Dillon hissed. The ravens swarmed in and dragged them over. Dillon couldn't hide his evil smile. His plan had been executed to the letter. "It was almost too easy."

Ryker tried to look defiant. "You've won a battle but you'll never win the war."

Dillon threw his head back and laughed menacingly. "If it's cliché time, try: 'The game is up. You've drawn dead'."

Ryker shook his head. "I'll never bow to you."

"Oh, you will," Dillon promised. "I guarantee it, especially when you find out what I can do to your precious Safi." He turned and walked away. "Come," he said over one shoulder, "see for yourself."

The ravens herded Ryker and Naz into the far corner of the barn.

Dillon marched over to Safiyya's cage. "I've only got to raise the partition."

Ryker suddenly noticed that her cage was linked to the mangy old falcon's. He struggled with his captors, but he was powerless against six of them. "Please don't, Dillon!"

124

he cried.

The raven cranked the handle half a turn and the old falcon tried to slip through the gap, but he was a little too big. "I've reduced you to begging already," the raven smirked. "You're so weak."

"If it was just you and me," Ryker said quietly, a small measure of control returning. "I'd tear you apart."

The raven smiled. "But it isn't, is it?"

Ryker was about to reply when the barn door was thrown open. Nigel marched in carrying the huge inert form of the eagle over one shoulder. He held the door open with his foot while the ravens corralled Eadric, Cuthbert, Hatcher and Hawkins. They looked at Ryker and shook their heads apologetically.

Nigel dumped Seamus in a large cage. "Hook, line and sinker. Throw the rest of them in cages next door." He turned to Dillon. "Leave her for now. We've more important things to attend to."

The ravens dragged Ryker and the others into the next stable. He looked longingly after Safi. She was crying, all hope of escape lost. The gamekeeper slammed the door behind them and locked him in a cage next to his parents. His father looked him over and shook his head, the pain endured while locked in the vice still evident on his face.

"You shouldn't have come," Algar said coldly. "It was obviously a trap."

Ryker ignored him. He hadn't seen his mother for days and tears were welling in his eyes. "Are you okay, Mum?"

Mercia twisted to face him and gasped when she saw the scratches on his head and chest. "You're hurt!"

"I'm fine," Ryker replied sullenly.

Mercia could tell his pride had been dented and that he wasn't seriously injured. She turned to her husband. "Give it a rest, Algar. Can't you see that he's been trying his best?"

"I couldn't leave you here," Ryker said. "Nigel's been selling falcon eggs to the zoo for a new enclosure. I'm pretty sure he has plans for us too."

Algar shook his head angrily. "I've never heard such rubbish. He only wants us out of the way so that the ravens can take over Redlands."

"There's much more to it than that," Cuthbert replied. "Ryker is right about the bird park."

"And he's been the bond that has kept us all together," Naz added, wondering if he'd heard a faint noise at the window. He cocked his head and listened again. "You should be proud of him."

"I can't see what good he's done," Algar scoffed. "You speak of this spirit of co-operation but it hasn't worked because now we're all trapped here. Face it, you've failed."

Naz didn't reply because he was sure there was something at the window. It opened a fraction of an inch and the fox poked her head inside. Algar's cold and aloof exterior began to crumble. He backed into Mercia and squeezed her tightly against the cage as if that would help. The fox leaped onto the floor, stood on her hind legs and lifted a set of keys from a hook by the door. Then she passed them through the bars to Ryker.

He selected one and slotted it into the lock. The cage door swung open and he smiled at his father. "What were you saying about co-operation not producing results?"

"We'll talk about this later," Algar replied. "Open the door."

Ryker slipped a key into the lock and released his parents. They were so relieved to be free that they slumped to the floor to catch their breath. Mercia threw her wings around her son and pulled him close but Algar quickly regained his composure and stood alone.

Ryker eventually freed himself from his mother's embrace and turned to Lufu. "Does that make us even?"

The fox grinned. "There's no need to keep score."

"Where are the others?" Ryker asked.

"They're waiting outside," she replied, leaping back onto the sill. "Let's get a move on before Dillon comes back. I overheard Nigel telling him to round up his flock for the final assault."

Ryker followed her into the night and joined Safiyya on the roof. He gave her a reassuring hug, tears rolling down their cheeks. "Thank God you're okay," he whispered at last. "What's Nigel done with the chicks?"

"I haven't seen my eggs since we got here," she whimpered.

"We haven't got time to look for them now," Algar said.

Ryker shook his head. "I'm not leaving without them." He looked around and noticed some of the flock was missing. "Where are Hawkins and Hatcher?"

Eadric shrugged. "As soon as Lufu freed them they headed south."

"So much for calling themselves friends," Algar muttered.

"They must have had a reason," Ryker countered, squaring up to his father.

Cuthbert stepped between them to keep the peace. "I'm afraid I agree with your father. We must regroup in Redlands before Dillon reappears."

Ryker stoutly refused to budge. "I will not abandon them again."

A distant cawing grew steadily louder from the direction of the field.

Safiyya looked at Ryker and bowed. "We'll have to come back for them."

"What about Seamus?" Naz asked. "We need him too."

"There's nothing we can do for him," Cuthbert said, the urgency in his voice rousing them to action. "We must leave now!"

"Night vision wins the day," Naz said, leaping into the air and skirting the woods to avoid running into the ravens before they were ready. "Make sure you keep up!"

As they flew over the gamekeeper's garden, a set of car headlights approached the main house.

16

It had been dusk and Gordon was halfway across the field when he heard a soft pop from the undergrowth by the fence separating his and Nigel's land. He guessed what it was and his fears were confirmed when he saw Seamus trying to peck the tranquilliser dart from his flank. The eagle couldn't reach it and began to weave drunkenly through the air until he eventually crash landed just inside the Ravenswood boundary. Gordon swore under his breath and ran back to his farm as the light began to fade.

He propped the shotgun by the back door and took off his boots. As he turned the door handle, he noticed a plastic bag in the wood basket. He opened it, took out a disc and frowned. He had other things on his mind but his curiosity got the better of him and he popped it into the computer in his study.

Ten minutes later, with the weight of the world on his shoulders, Gordon was racing up to the animal sanctuary. His car screeched to a halt in front of the main building and he leaped out as Simone was leaving for the night.

"I just saw Nigel shoot that eagle," he gasped.

She threw her hands up and glared at him. "I thought we'd been through this."

He gripped her shoulders, anguish in his eyes. "What will it take for you to believe me?"

"The truth," she said flatly

Gordon stood back, sincerity replacing anguish. "Relationships are based on trust," he said quietly. "Come with me to Nigel's. If I'm wrong, you'll never hear another bad word about him."

Simone looked at him with renewed respect. "Shouldn't we call the police first?"

Gordon tapped his pocket and held the car door open. "I've got my phone if there's trouble."

They climbed in and he accelerated out of the car park. Nothing was said on the way to Nigel's. They were clearly both confused by what was happening.

A few minutes later, Gordon pulled up to the gates guarding Nigel's estate and opened his window. "Do you know the code?"

Simone shook her head. "Try the last four digits of his phone number."

"Let's hope he's that stupid," Gordon replied. He punched in the code on a keypad and the gates opened. "Never in doubt." He drove up the long drive and parked in front of the gamekeeper's dilapidated farmhouse as the birds flew overhead. He climbed out and knocked on the door.

Nigel eventually answered, and he was clearly agitated. "How did you get through the gate?" he spat.

"It wasn't difficult to guess the code," Gordon replied. "You've got no imagination so any idiot could have done it."

"Thanks," Simone said, smiling when she saw the look on his face. "It's alright. I know you didn't mean it like that."

Gordon squeezed her hand. "Good."

Suitably insulted, the gamekeeper leaned forward until his face was only an inch from Gordon's. "What do you want?"

"I'd like to know what happened to that eagle," the farmer replied. He was finding it hard not to lose his temper but knew it'd only give Nigel the upper hand.

The gamekeeper shrugged. "I've no idea what you're talking about."

"I saw you shoot it, Nigel," Gordon replied. "So there's

no need to continue lying."

Simone slipped her arm through Gordon's. "Is it true, Nigel?"

The gamekeeper shook his head angrily. "I don't know anything about a golden eagle!"

Gordon stood his ground, a thin smile forming. "No one said anything about it being golden."

Simone backed away towards the car. "Let's call the police. They can deal with this now."

Nigel reached behind the front door and pulled out his shotgun.

"Simone, meet what's responsible for all the injured pheasants," Gordon said.

"How could I have been so ignorant?" she whispered.

Nigel held the gun across his chest and flicked the safety catch off with his thumb.

"Don't even think about it, Nigel," Gordon said flatly.

"Then don't force me too," the gamekeeper replied. "Now, get off my land!"

Keeping one eye on Nigel, they climbed back into the car and sped off down the drive. Simone was trembling. "I'm so sorry I doubted you. What are we going to do?"

"Exactly as you suggested," Gordon replied. "We're going to call the police because there's far more to this than meets the eye."

Nigel threw open the door to the barn, shotgun at the ready. "Say your prayers," he barked, raising the gun and marching inside. He suddenly noticed some of the cages were empty. "Where are you?" he roared, slamming the door and charging back outside.

Dillon and his flock flooded into the yard.

Nigel could barely contain himself. "They've escaped! Hunt them down and annihilate them. I want every bird in Redlands Forest dead by morning!"

Dillon leaped off the gatepost, his flock swarming through the trees behind him.

Ryker was the last to land by the stream. The others were already trotting along the faint path to the clearing. It was eerily quiet and he glanced over his shoulder at the woods on the other side of the field. His heart sank when he saw a wave of birds massing in the sky above. He was quite adept at picking birds out by their silhouettes and saw that the ravens and cuckoos had another ally. He charged into the forest and soon caught the others.

"What is it?" Cuthbert asked, dread rising in his stomach when he clocked Ryker's expression.

Ryker cocked his head towards the field. "They're getting ready to invade. They'll overwhelm us with superior numbers. And I spotted a magpie amongst them."

"Not Jolenta," Wilbur groaned. "She's the devil incarnate."

Cuthbert sprang into action and began barking orders like a machinegun. Some of Wilbur's military know-how must have rubbed off on him. "If you control the air, you dictate the battle. They're forcing our hand by breaking our territorial agreement again but if we respond with everything we've got then we can defeat them."

"We're going to need your help, Dad," Ryker said.

Algar sighed and bowed his head, then took a deep breath. It was time to clear the air so they were united in battle. "I'm surprised you're still talking to me."

"All I ever wanted was for you to believe in me," Ryker replied quietly. "But in your eyes I was never good enough and that hurts."

Algar knew where the conversation was going but he had to get it off his chest. "I shouldn't have left you in charge of the nest when you were so young. I should've taken responsibility for what happened but I blamed you

132

to justify my own grief. It was a terrible thing to do, and I'm very sorry."

Ryker felt some of the moment's tension falling away. "I still could have saved her if I'd learned how to hunt. So I can't forgive myself yet."

"Don't make the same mistake I did and keep it buttoned up inside," Algar warned. "If you come to terms with it, you can grieve and move on."

Ryker smiled thinly. "Let's cope together then."

Algar drew his son close, the simple gesture saying everything.

"I hate to break up the family reunion," Naz interrupted, "but the ravens are on their way."

Safiyya nuzzled into Ryker's neck, a look of determination on her face. "You'll have the chicks on your side tonight. Fight for us all."

"I will," he replied, holding her tightly. "You'll be safe here with Wilbur."

Ryker released her and turned to the others. "Naz and I will fly together. The same goes for mum and dad."

"And Eadric and I'll finish the ravens off if they fall into the field or get too close," Cuthbert added. "We can tend to injuries on our side too."

Ryker waved to Safiyya and led the others back down the path to the field. They were quiet, their nerves clearly getting the better of them. When they reached the stream the scale of the attack became clear. There were perhaps two dozen ravens and as many cuckoos circling above. They'd chased off the remaining birds as if clearing the battleground.

Ryker gathered them under the oak so they couldn't be seen from the air. "There's no time for a pep talk so let's make sure we're there for each other."

Ryker and Naz leaped into the air. Their hand had been forced and they were heavily outnumbered, but they hoped superior tactics and determination would win the day. Four birds dived to intercept them. Flint the cuckoo immediately pulled up and turned back. To face these two head on was suicidal. One of the ravens also saw sense but the other two continued their misguided attack. Ryker bared his beak and lashed out with his talons as they passed. He missed the cuckoo but the raven took a razor sharp claw full in the face, snapping its head back and killing it instantly.

Naz skilfully avoided the cuckoo and turned sharply to strike himself. He was far more manoeuvrable and ripped a couple of the bird's tail feathers loose before it broke free. Now they were up amongst the flock. He and Ryker soon developed a strategy to even things up a bit. The owl, a fearsome predator in its own right, herded the cuckoos towards Ryker like a collie corralling the sheep. Between them they managed to down another two birds.

They continued to climb, but the magpie was circling even higher. They ignored her for now. The initial skirmishes were going their way and she posed no immediate threat. Ryker remembered the advice given to him by the jackdaw and finally felt comfortable in his element. Not even the nervous tension in his chest could stop him from exacting revenge.

He singled out a solitary cuckoo in the moonlight and rolled into a stooping dive. The wind rushed by his face, his neck feathers ruffling up and billowing out. He knew Naz was close behind and would finish off the attack if he only wounded the bird. Their strategy was so simple: they would stick together regardless, targeting one bird at a time. Ryker closed at a staggering speed. He angled his beak to strike at the bird's neck and connected ferociously. The cuckoo was almost torn apart by the attack.

Algar drew alongside looking particularly pleased. "I see you've mastered the art," he said proudly.

Ryker smiled and let him take the credit. "I had a good teacher."

"There are so many of them," Algar replied seriously. "You must watch your back."

Ryker nodded as he rolled away to his right and struck at another cuckoo. He then pulled up and rejoined Naz behind a raven. Things had started off well for the Redlands birds, but their good fortune was about to change.

Nigel crouched in the hide and panned a night scope across the battleground. The four birds of prey were dispatching his ravens and cuckoos with apparent ease. He turned to Dillon. "They must be getting tired now. Lead the rest of your flock into battle, and remember to split them up."

Dillon leaped into the trees. The full moon cast its rays through the branches and bathed the field in a surreal glow. He marshalled his forces and waited until the owl strayed too close to the fence. Then he jumped off the branch and raced to intercept him.

Naz saw him coming and broke off to engage him but two cuckoos distracted him by cutting in front of him before bolting for the fence. Naz's killer instinct got the better of him and he gave chase, leaving Ryker to fend for himself. Ryker called after him but he was too engrossed in the hunt to hear.

As they closed to within fifty yards, Nigel placed his night glasses on the ground and picked up the shotgun. The crafty cuckoos were leading the owl into his trap. He didn't have to wait long for them to come into range. The cuckoos swooped over the fence and the owl followed. Nigel raised the gun to his shoulder and sighted on all three birds. He wasn't at all concerned that he might strike the cuckoos. The briefest of opportunities arose and he squeezed the trigger.

The report was deafening in the hide. Smoke and fire burst from the muzzle and an angry swarm of metal shot struck the birds. All three tumbled to the ground. Nigel unloaded the second barrel at them as they fell. There were only three more birds standing between his flock and mastery of the air. He allowed himself a satisfied smile as he ejected the two cartridges and reloaded. Soon it would all be over.

Ryker heard the report and broke off an attack on one of the cuckoos. He was halfway to the fence when he noticed Eadric whipping below him to check on Naz. The distraction cost Ryker. He heard a loud hissing and then Dillon and another raven collided with him and wrestled him towards the ground. They pecked at his eyes and tried to tear out his feathers.

He fought back like a bird possessed, striking out with his sharp talons and ferocious beak. He got lucky and stabbed one of the ravens in the chest, but Dillon ripped out a clump of his feathers and he lost control. The raven knew it was a serious injury and broke off his attack to watch the inevitable crash. Ryker desperately tried to right himself but ended up tumbling into the field and landing hard on his head.

Ryker rolled over in the grass and moaned. The impact had rattled his bones. He could hardly move but eventually managed to sit up. Dillon's strikes weren't as serious as he'd first thought: he'd only removed a couple of feathers and thrown him off balance. The scratches on his underbelly were also superficial but he plucked some grass to clean them anyway.

"Are you alright?" Cuthbert asked as he parted the long grass and joined him. "That was some fall."

"Just winded I think," Ryker replied, "but they've taken a chunk out of my tail."

Cuthbert examined his injuries and shrugged. "I'll have to remove a couple more feathers I'm afraid." He glanced upwards at the sound of wings but it was only

Mercia flying cover. She was obviously checking on her son and protecting them from further attack. "You'll have to compromise on manoeuvrability," Cuthbert added as he carefully plucked his tail feathers until they were even. He knew it was painful because Ryker flinched but he'd clenched his beak and didn't make a sound. "Right, let's get you back into the fray," the pheasant said eventually.

Ryker shook himself down. "Thanks, Cuthbert. How are we doing? It looks like Naz took one for the team."

The old pheasant knew he had to tell him the truth. "Eadric is checking on him but he was hit by the shotgun so it doesn't look good.

"What about my parents?" Ryker asked.

Cuthbert cocked his head. "Your mum's your guardian angel at the moment, but I haven't seen your dad for a while. I'm afraid he might be down too."

Ryker shook his head defiantly. "We'll keep going until there are none of us left." Then he squeezed the pheasant's shoulder. "Retreat into the forest if you have to but don't let them take any of us alive, and that includes Safi." His point made, Ryker flapped hard to compensate for his missing feathers and leaped into the air to rejoin the battle.

Naz opened his eyes and gasped with pain. One of his wings was pinned under his body and he couldn't move. He was about to give up when Eadric knelt beside him.

The cockerel quickly assessed the situation. "You've taken some shot under your left wing. It hasn't penetrated too deeply by the looks of things."

The owl grimaced. "Can you get to it?"

"It might hurt a bit," Eadric said, not waiting for a reply. He simply had to get Naz back in the air. He slowly lifted the owl's wing and saw the hole made by the ball-bearing. He eased his beak into the wound and plucked the shot out.

Naz tensed and held his breath. When it was over he let out a sigh and stood, flexing the wing to check he could still fly. There was a little blood but it soon clotted and the pain subsided into a dull ache. "That's much better, Eadric. You'd make a great nurse."

The cockerel looked pleased and bowed. "You know where I am if you need me."

Naz took to the air to resume the fight, the adrenalin surge masking his pain. He joined Algar as the huge falcon dispatched yet another raven with his lethal talons. "Stay away from the fence," the owl shouted. "Nigel's hidden in the bushes with a shotgun."

Algar nodded and led them back towards the chalk cliffs but he was clearly tiring. "We'll draw the cuckoos over here so Ryker can take them out."

As the moon rose higher into the night sky the outcome was still in the balance. Ryker dived down the cliff face towards two ravens that were attacking his mother. He swiped at one with his feet and knocked it to the ground, then gouged the second with his beak. The jet black bird realised it was about to get eaten and bolted for the fence.

Ryker and Naz joined Mercia and they landed on the cliff for a breather. They noticed that the magpie still hadn't entered the fray. She was circling high above and issuing orders but refusing to take part. Ryker guessed she had no stomach for the battle and was waiting for their defeat before joining the winners and claiming the plaudits.

"Where's dad?" he gasped.

"We got separated amongst the ravens," Mercia replied.

"He was right behind me a minute ago," Naz said. "He might have landed further up the cliff."

"We must find him," Ryker said quietly. "He's our only hope."

Just then, Nigel's shotgun spat fire from the hide to their left. Through the smoke a falcon appeared. It was Algar! And he was clearly wounded. Ryker and Naz leaped off the cliff to help him but they were still a hundred yards away when he was set upon by three more birds, including Flint and the merciless Dillon. Algar's tail feathers billowed out behind him and he flipped into a forward somersault and tumbled towards the ground.

"Dad!" Ryker shouted.

He looked around for support but his dive had taken him away from the others. He was going to have to rescue his father on his own, but Algar was spiralling out of control. If he crashed at that speed he might be killed. Ryker glanced over his shoulder and accelerated hard. He knew there was little Naz could do because he was too small, but he was racing after them both anyway.

Ryker soon caught Algar and gripped him tightly around the neck. He flapped as hard as he could to try to slow their descent but he wasn't powerful enough. Even with Naz's help they couldn't prevent the inevitable. Ryker opened his mouth to shout a warning but no sound came. The last thing he saw was long grass waving in a gentle breeze as it rushed out of the darkness to meet them.

The impact winded him and they all tumbled into a heap by the stream. Algar rolled forward, smashed his head on a tree stump and lay still; Naz cried out in pain as the huge falcon rolled on top of him and crushed one of his feet; Ryker was thrown off to one side, his head spinning, his eyesight fading.

In one fell swoop the battle had been lost.

Ryker eventually stirred and lifted his head. It was darker than when they'd crashed so he must have been knocked out. He took a deep breath to clear the cobwebs and stood. Naz was massaging his broken foot while the skies above were being over-flown by ravens squawking triumphantly. Cuthbert and Eadric joined them, their faces grim. Wilbur and Safiyya also appeared. Their brave defence of the farm had been in vain.

Ryker suddenly noticed that his father hadn't moved and joined his mother by his side. She was shaking her head and whimpering as if in a trance. Ryker knelt to check on Algar. There was a streak of blood running across the top of his head where the shotgun blast had hit, and there were scratches all over his body. There was also a huge lump behind his ear.

Ryker leaned close. "Dad, can you hear me?"

There was no reply. Algar's eyes were open but sightless.

"Please take a look at him, Cuthbert," Ryker begged.

All the other birds crowded round as Cuthbert began his examination.

The pheasant listened to Algar's chest to check if he was breathing but after nearly a minute he stood back. "I'm sorry," he said, putting a wing around Ryker's shoulders. "He's gone."

"What do you mean?" Mercia cried. "He can't be. Please do something!"

Cuthbert led Ryker to the stream's edge and bowed his head. "I'm so sorry, my boy."

Ryker's mind was whirling uncontrollably but he suddenly came to his senses and ran back to his father's body. He collapsed on the ground next to him and beat his chest with his wings, tears rolling down his cheeks. He wiped the blood from around his father's mouth and pleaded with him. "Come on, Dad, fight," he implored. "I know you're still there!"

Mercia put her wings around her son and pulled him away. "It's okay, Ryker," she murmured. "Leave him."

Ryker broke free and pounded his chest again, then crumpled to the ground and nuzzled into his father's body sobbing softly.

17

MP Craig Biggs shuffled a stack of papers on his desk in his parliamentary office and checked his watch. It was late. He had to meet Nigel in the car park in an hour's time, but traffic at this time on a Friday should be light.

He pulled on a rumpled grey business jacket, which barely made it round his flabby middle, and finished a mug of coffee. He wiped a few drops from his bushy grey beard with the back of his hand and dropped the papers into a worn leather briefcase. As he opened the door and flipped off the lights, his desk phone rang.

Biggs wanted to ignore it but eventually sat down in the half light streaming in from the corridor and picked up the receiver. "What can I do for you?" he asked in the gruff voice that Nigel so despised.

The foreign voice on the other end of the line was cold, calculating, and spoke with an efficiency of words that left no room for misinterpretation or doubt. "I assume our deal is still on."

"Of course," Biggs replied. "The money has cleared so I'm picking up Nigel's falcons tonight. You've plenty of time to ship them out of the country before the competition next week. As agreed, I'm having the eggs taken to the zoo for the new enclosure."

"I don't believe you."

Biggs noticed his office door was slowly swinging shut, the shaft of light from the corridor shrinking around him. Sweat appeared on his brow and dripped into his eye. "You have my word, Omar, as a respected MP."

"There's no such thing," Omar replied caustically.

"I know you're lying but I'll give you until tomorrow morning to deliver the falcons. My flight leaves at nine. Goodnight."

Biggs loosened his tie, his face pale, and hung up. The office door clicked shut with a degree of finality, leaving the MP alone in the dark.

18

How long Ryker lay next to his father he couldn't remember, but he suddenly felt movement inside his chest. He sat bolt upright and leaned closer. It was the faint thump of Algar's heart. Ryker leaped to his feet and gazed into his eyes.

"I knew you were still with us," he whispered. The other birds were still gathered in defeat and hadn't noticed what was happening but Ryker didn't want to raise their hopes yet so he kept his voice down. "Fight it, Dad. Come back to us."

Algar twitched and the light returned to his eyes. "Did we win?" he rasped groggily, rolling over and shaking his head to clear it.

"Not yet," Ryker said. He then turned to the others and announced proudly: "He's still alive!"

Mercia rushed over and hugged them. "I'm sorry I doubted you, Ryker. You knew he'd pull through." She stood back, the tears still welling in her eyes. "Careful now, darling."

Algar slowly stood but his legs were a little wobbly. "It's okay, dear. The shot only grazed my head."

Ryker stretched his wings and realised he was still in pretty good shape. "I'm going back up."

Cuthbert shook his head. "This doesn't change anything. It'd be suicide to go it alone."

"I promised Safi I'd defend her with my life," Ryker said flatly. "And I intend to honour that commitment. If we're going down, we're going down fighting."

"I'll go with you, boss," Naz said grittily. "I don't need

my feet while I'm in the air. Sitting around is only making them more painful."

"You'll get yourselves killed," Algar said quietly. "Surrender and we still have our lives in front of us."

"I'll not live by Dillon's rules," Ryker countered.

"Ryker, please!" Algar insisted.

"Sorry, Dad," Ryker said firmly, "but you're going to have to trust me."

Cuthbert was about to continue the protest when Hatcher flew in low and landed next to the stream. "Sorry I'm late. We got a bit lost."

"Surprise, surprise," Naz muttered.

"We?" Ryker said.

Hatcher pointed upwards. "I brought the cavalry."

They craned their necks and their mouths dropped open. Hawkins, Asketil and two more birds from the airport ploughed into the ravens with a vengeance. They scattered and two dropped from the sky.

Naz's mouth dropped open. "Wonders will never cease."

What had been a pessimistic camp five seconds earlier was now buoyed by the good news. Some of their confidence returned and the pain from their injuries faded.

"I found someone else too," Hatcher said proudly.

They all turned at the heavy beat of wings. Seamus burst from the trees above them and tore into the Ravenswood flock. He screeched loudly and swiped his huge talons at the enemy birds.

Algar nodded slowly. "This does change things. I'm with you, son."

"No," Mercia said. "You're hurt."

"I'll not chicken out of a good old-fashioned scrap," he replied.

Ryker hugged his father again. "Let's finish them off."

He trotted back into the field and leaped into the air,

confident that with Hawkins and Seamus helping they could still beat the Ravenswood birds. He reached the flock in no time and singled out one of the cuckoos. Flint was fighting a kestrel and didn't see him coming. Ryker lined him up and struck his underbelly hard. Flint screeched in pain but the falcon's beak had mortally wounded him. He gasped and his eyes rolled into the back of his head. He was dead long before he hit the ground.

"Nice work, buddy," Hawkins shouted. "There are only a dozen of them left now."

"I thought you'd deserted us," Ryker replied, his confidence continuing to build.

"Be serious," Hawkins scoffed.

Ryker rolled onto one side and joined Hawkins in formation. They set off after a raven together. The large black bird desperately tried to shake them by running for the fence, but Ryker closed it down and struck before they strayed too close to Nigel. They then swung onto the tail of another.

Suddenly three jackdaws broke in front of them and downed the raven.

"Couldn't 'ave you taking all the glory, could I?" one shouted over his shoulder.

Ryker frowned. "I didn't expect to see you again."

Duke shrugged. "Them ravens get everywhere. Sooner we get rid of 'em the better."

"How did you know?" Ryker asked.

Duke was about to reply when one of his sons broke away and dived after a cuckoo. He winked at Ryker and then he was gone.

Ryker shook his head and rejoined Hawkins as Naz dispatched a cuckoo with a barrel roll. "Show off!" he shouted.

Naz looped the loop while saluting with one wing. "Years of practice!"

Seamus and Algar drew alongside in an arrowhead

146

formation and they tore into the remaining ravens. The Ravenswood flock were now outnumbered and there was no chance of them defeating the Redlands birds. United only in defeat, they realised they'd failed and scattered to all corners of the compass.

Dillon skilfully evaded Seamus and swooped down to the hide. He landed next to the gamekeeper and shuffled nervously.

Nigel fixed him with a stare that should have had him thinking about his own safety. "You had surprise and superior numbers on your side but you still blew it," he hissed angrily, flicking off the shotgun's safety catch. "These woods may bear your name but you'll not be around to preside over them. You know the price of failure."

The raven suddenly realised what was about to happen. He saw Nigel's finger squeezing the trigger and he leaped off the perch to escape but he was too late. The shotgun blast ripped him to shreds and his remains fell to the ground.

Nigel crawled out of the hide and jogged back to the house.

Thirty yards away Jolenta had been keeping an eye on the situation. She watched Dillon's demise with interest. She'd never considered them competitors but with the other birds out of the way she needed to kindle a relationship with Nigel that would have its rewards for both of them. She flitted over to the hide and started pecking the loose flesh from Dillon's body.

The gamekeeper crossed the yard and slammed his front door. He opened a security panel in the cupboard under the stairs and made sure the fences were electrified and the gates were locked. It would be almost impossible to break into the farm now but he reloaded the shotgun just in case. He then marched into the kitchen and took the two falcon eggs out of the holdall on the end of the cooker. He stared blankly at them for a moment before wrapping them in a tea towel and putting them in a Tupperware container. He popped the lot into his jacket pocket and slipped out into the yard.

Ryker landed in the field by the stream under a full moon. The other birds were whooping and cheering. Seamus clapped him on the back while Hawkins gripped him with both wings and threw his head back in delight. Cuthbert, Eadric, Duke, Hatcher, Wilbur, Mercia, Safiyya and Asketil were all applauding. Ryker didn't quite know what to make of it all and his cheeks flushed with embarrassment. It had taken a huge effort but they'd finally banished the ravens and cuckoos from the forest.

"I hate to break up the party," Cuthbert said, "but we're not out of the woods just yet."

Hatcher looked around. "Clearly."

Ryker cut their celebrations short with a wave of his wings. "We need to free the birds that Nigel has been holding and find our eggs."

Safiyya held him tight. "This time I'm coming with you."

Ryker shook his head. "You'll be safer at Gordon's."

"Take Hawkins, Naz, Seamus and Hatcher with you," Cuthbert said. "We'll wait for you at Gordon's and make sure he calls the police."

"Be careful, my boy," Algar said. "Don't take any chances while he's still armed."

"Bring them home," Safiyya added.

Ryker embraced her for a long time. "Don't worry, darling, by the morning this will all be over." He gave her an affectionate squeeze and took a deep breath, the pain from his injuries already fading. "We'll soon be a family again."

He checked the other birds were ready and took to the air. Naz drew alongside, his expert vision indispensable, and the five of them ghosted across the field, scene of the bloody battle only an hour earlier. It was peaceful now and the pale silver moon cast a soft luminescence across their backs. They all felt the nerves as they approached the Ravenswood estate and entered the unknown once more.

"Don't land anywhere until we're inside the yard," Ryker said, passing on his father's warning. He'd ignored his advice a couple of times but because he couldn't be sure if the mythical beast existed it was prudent to exercise caution. "We'll meet on the barn roof."

"Follow me," Hatcher said, taking over the lead. "It's where the gamekeeper used to keep the homing pigeons."

"We've finally found somewhere you know how to get to," Naz said.

They followed the pigeon through the woods and into the forbidding courtyard. It was deathly quiet below and pitch black to boot. Ryker landed on the barn next to Hatcher and shuddered. His nerves tingled as if the temperature had dropped several degrees, but he knew it was just tension. They were inside the lion's den and his senses were on full alert.

"Hawkins will be a useful lookout with his ultraviolet vision," Ryker whispered. "Wait here with Seamus and Hatcher while Naz and I see what we can do."

He and Naz dropped into the darkness. The yard was dirty and mud seeped through the gaps between their talons. Ryker listened for trouble but there was nothing. He'd been expecting a battery of searchlights to come on and Nigel to appear with his gun. Thankfully it was still quiet.

Naz followed him to the huge barn where the rare birds were kept. The door was unlocked so they wedged their feet behind it and pulled it open. It squeaked on rusty hinges and they froze. They waited to be sure Nigel wasn't setting a trap before filing inside. An acidic but not unpleasant smell assaulted their nostrils. Naz tried to wrinkle up his beak to identify it but it was alien to him.

A hundred rare birds were crammed into tiny cages. Ryker hopped between them and glanced down the aisle. Nigel was sloshing liquid across the floor at the far end of the barn from a large red can. He and Naz looked at each other and shrugged. When Nigel reached the far door, he dropped the can in the next barn, then lit a match and dropped it into the liquid. The petrol ignited with a loud whoosh and quickly spread into the aisles. Nigel laughed and disappeared while the birds squawked in terror and rattled their cages.

Ryker and Naz knew they didn't have time to free all the birds but they grabbed two sets of keys hanging from the nail by the door and opened the cages as fast as they could. The fire spread rapidly and was soon licking at their feathers. Like birds possessed, they raced up and down the aisles throwing open cage doors and ushering the rare species outside.

They eventually came to the last aisle. It was going to be close. The fire was rising up the walls and blackening the beams above them. Smoke billowed from the doorway as Ryker inserted a key into the last cage. He was choking on the fumes now.

"Hurry!" an illegally imported red-tailed hawk implored.

"I am trying, you know," Ryker gasped, fumbling with the key as visibility deteriorated.

He finally managed to open the door and the hawk nodded politely before disappearing into the gloom. Ryker looked for Naz but he couldn't see him for smoke. With his feathers smouldering and his skin singed, Ryker battled through the flames and burst through the stable door as if fired from a cannon.

Naz was just landing on the roof opposite but Ryker had other things to worry about. His feathers had ignited so he angled low across the yard and dived headfirst towards a water trough. "Out of the fire!" he gasped, plunging into the icy water. When he resurfaced, he heard a strange sizzling sound and steam burst around him. "And into the frying pan."

He crawled out of the trough looking somewhat bedraggled and shook himself down. His feathers quickly dried and fluffed up to twice their normal size. He saw the others laughing but Naz suddenly stopped and cocked his head. Ryker was about to join them on the roof when a torch beam pinned him to the wall. Nigel had crept round behind the barns using the shadow from the fire as cover and had taken him by surprise.

He shouldered the shotgun and took careful aim. "Well, well," he hissed, "look who came home to roost! It's time to put you out of my misery."

Naz spotted the danger and silently dropped off the roof. He waited until he was only a couple of feet from Nigel's ear before emitting an ear-splitting screech. The gamekeeper threw one hand up to his head and spun round. He tripped over a feed trough, lost his footing and overbalanced into the mud.

Ryker followed Naz into the air and they alit on the roof of the main house. "Back where he belongs," he gasped. "Grovelling in the mud."

Naz nodded to several sets of swirling blue lights in the distance. "Gordon must have called the police," he said smugly. "They can deal with Nigel now."

The gamekeeper swore loudly and staggered to his feet. He was covered in a revolting mixture of mud and manure. He tried to clean the torch but only succeeded in wiping more muck over the lens. Then he noticed the stable door was open. He stuck his head round it in the hope that the birds were all going up in flames but the cages were empty.

"No!" he gasped. "My insurance money!"

At that instant two police cars pulled into the courtyard and skidded to a stop in the mud.

"Stop right there and put your hands on your head," a policeman shouted as he climbed out and knelt behind the car door. "You are covered by armed police."

Nigel lowered the weapon to his side, a look of defiance on his face. "You have no right to be on this property," he hissed. "Leave now or face the consequences."

"This is your last chance!" the policeman barked. "Put the weapon down!"

"Put it down, Nigel," Gordon said. He climbed out of the back seat and held his hands up in a gesture of peace. "Let's go inside and talk this through."

A cold rage welled in the gamekeeper's stomach as the story became clear. "So this is your way of taking over my farm, is it? I would have expected better from you, Gordon."

"Take a look at yourself, Nigel," the farmer said quietly. "You've been after my land for years but I refused to sell so you hatched a plan to force me out. The game, as they say, is up. And as for taking over your farm," he said, gesturing at the fire, "I think you've taken care of that."

"You have no idea what you're getting into," Nigel said, hoping to gain the upper hand and catch everyone off guard. "This goes way beyond what you see here."

"I'm aware of that," Gordon replied. "You've been stealing falcon eggs from the chalk cliffs for a while now. I couldn't catch you in the act of course – you were far too clever for that – but I knew it went on all the same. The trouble is you made a mistake taking that last batch of eggs because these falcons were so committed to their

152

family that they decided to fight back."

"Nonsense!" Nigel scoffed. "Are you telling me that they're intelligent?"

"They discovered that you were selling the eggs to Feathered-Friends for a huge profit," Gordon continued. "That's how you've been financing your other little project, but we'll come to that in a moment. The birds learned all about your illegal dealings, and about the dreadful conditions on your farm. They also discovered your nasty little secret at the lab." Gordon noticed that Nigel's blustery defiance was fast evaporating. He was being confronted with cold hard facts that would put him in prison for a long time. "Am I getting warm?" he asked sarcastically.

Another police car pulled up and Simone climbed out.

Nigel fixed her with an acid stare. "I might have known you'd be involved. Very cosy."

"To think I almost trusted you," she replied. "What a mistake that would have been."

Nigel ignored her. "So these remarkable birds will testify, will they, Gordon?" he said, throwing his head back and laughing maniacally. "'Yes, your honour, squawk, squawk!' You'll never prove anything! I'm surprised you still think this was about the falcon eggs."

The tension in the air was palpable as Simone slipped her hand through Gordon's and gave it a squeeze. "You'd better tell him what he already knows," she whispered.

The farmer drew her close and took a deep breath. He was worried about what Nigel might do but there were a number of armed officers spreading out around the yard so he held up the disc. "The police have everything they need here, Nigel: details of all your financial dealings over the past seven years; a complete list of your animal rights violations; and the name of your source in government, which they'll confirm using your computer records. You've been selling rare eggs to the lab at Feathered-Friends for cosmetic testing to try to pay off the enormous outstanding mortgage on your estate. Then there's the small matter of your chain of supply to the local supermarkets. The area manager told me earlier that you'd agreed to drop your chicken prices to undercut me. You'd have taken a good share of my business, upped your offer on my farm and forced me out, which would have given you access to the cliffs and the nests – and therefore the eggs – of more migratory falcons. The cycle of greed and corruption would have continued and you might have become a very rich man. Now, when all this gets presented in court I'd say it makes a pretty convincing case against you, wouldn't you agree?"

Nigel was stunned. His plan had just unravelled in front of him. Thankfully they didn't seem to know anything about his other interests but there was still nowhere left to turn. The gun barrel dropped into the mud and his shoulders slumped forward.

One of the policemen inched across the yard. "Okay, Nigel, lay the gun down so we can all go home."

Nigel held the stock for the policeman to take.

Gordon knew the gamekeeper was doing the right thing. He turned to Simone and gave her a hug, his heartbeat slowing at last. She held him tight, the unbearable tension finally easing.

Suddenly Nigel raised the gun with one hand and pushed the policeman into the mud with the other. He sighted on the middle of Gordon's back and his finger curled around the trigger.

On the roof of the barn Ryker realised what was about to happen. He and Seamus leaped off simultaneously and raced towards the gamekeeper in a desperate attempt to save Gordon's life. Time seemed to slow down.

Ryker flew straight for Nigel's hand and spread his

talons to inflict maximum damage. He'd seen it work before so he also let out a blood-curdling screech. Nigel was momentarily distracted, which gave Ryker enough time to smash into the gun and knock it off line. His razor sharp talons raked across Nigel's hand and his beak tore a strip of flesh from his arm.

The gamekeeper roared with pain and tried to fend him off but the eagle then crashed into his back and he pitched forward. There was a deafening report as the gun went off and smoke billowed around them. Nigel dropped it in the mud and bolted for the woods, oblivious to the shouts of the policemen in the yard. He vaulted the gate with surprising agility and disappeared up the path like a shadow.

The policemen tore open the gate and gave chase, their torches flickering amongst the trees. Every so often they caught a glimpse of the gamekeeper as he tried to lose them in the woods but they were only thirty yards behind him when he got to the cliff.

Nigel glanced over his shoulder and started up the steep face. Every so often he slipped, sending lumps of chalk tumbling down on his pursuers, but he was soon twenty feet up and climbing strongly. The policemen fanned out along the footpath and took careful aim.

"Don't shoot," Gordon panted. "He's unarmed and can't escape."

All eyes returned to the cliffs but what happened next surprised them all.

Ryker burst out of the trees and raced up the cliff towards the gamekeeper. He was flying on cold rage now, the thought of what Nigel might have done to his eggs spurring him on. He reached the gamekeeper in a flash and struck at his head. Nigel tried to knock him away but he lost his footing and slid back a few feet. His pocket ripped open on a rocky outcrop and the Tupperware box containing the eggs fell out!

Ryker didn't notice and continued striking at him. Nigel swung an arm at his head but overbalanced and slipped back another ten feet. The Tupperware box dislodged its lid and the eggs tumbled down the last few feet.

Perched on Gordon's shoulder, Safiyya saw what was happening. "Ryker!" she screamed. "The eggs!"

Ryker's heart sank. The eggs bounced off the chalk, landed on the footpath and smashed. He gasped in shock and raced to their remains, his hopes in tatters. Gordon, Simone and the birds crowded round. Safiyya expected Ryker to be devastated but he turned at her approach and smiled broadly, then stood back. Two tiny white fluffy chicks crawled out of the shattered eggs.

"Oh, Ryker," Safi gasped. "They were ready to hatch!"

She picked them up and cradled them in her wings while Ryker pulled her close. The chicks looked up at them, opened their mouths and called for food. Tears formed in Safi's eyes.

"Beautiful," Ryker said softly. "They take after their mother."

"A family at last," Safi said. "Let's take them home."

A commotion to their right startled them. Nigel jumped down the last few feet and took advantage of the distraction to shoulder past the policemen and make a break for the woods.

"Will he never learn?" Gordon sighed.

The policemen turned and gave chase once more. They were tiring of the game but couldn't shoot an unarmed man. They all suddenly heard a loud scream from the woods and charged through the undergrowth to investigate.

The policemen entered the small clearing and raised their guns. Nigel was lying on his back while a huge black cat gripped him round the throat with its massive paws. The gamekeeper writhed in the mud and screamed in terror. The policemen crouched and aimed at the beast.

156

"Don't shoot!" Simone cried as she ran up to the police line. "I think she's tame."

"No chance, ma'am," one of the officers said, his voice quivering. "It's going to kill him."

Simone grabbed his arm. "Just give me a minute, will you? If she attacks either of us then you can shoot."

The policeman saw the look of determination in her eyes and recognised her from the Wildlife series on television. "I guess you can try," he said, lowering his gun to let her past.

Simone crouched to make herself appear less of a threat and inched into the clearing. Nigel had stopped screaming and now lay sobbing on the ground. The animal was gripping his jacket tightly around his neck with its extended claws. If the big cat felt so inclined it could easily finish him off with a bite to the throat or a simple suffocating grip but it was now focusing on Simone instead.

She edged closer. She was used to dealing with animals of all shapes and sizes but her heart was pounding. This was a very big cat and easily outweighed her. A bead of perspiration rolled into her eye and she blinked. She was within five yards of the cat now. Its eyes were a vivid and hypnotic yellow. She shook her head, took a deep breath and began talking to it in low, soothing tones.

After about a minute she was kneeling next to it. She ignored the petrified gamekeeper and reached out to stroke the animal. It responded to her touch and retracted its claws, then rubbed itself against her as if sensing her good intentions. Simone felt a bond of trust had been created. There was a thin metal collar around the cat's neck so she ran her hands along it until she found a tag. She couldn't believe her luck but the cat actually appeared to have a name. She glanced at the tag and smiled.

"Hello, Gytha," she whispered into its ear. "Can you let the man up now? There's a good girl."

The semi-wild cat appeared to think for a moment

before taking its paws off Nigel's chest. He staggered to his feet and fell into the arms of one of the policemen. They cuffed his hands behind his back and led him away.

Simone scratched the cat behind its ears. "Let's get you something nice to eat instead," she said, standing and backing away a couple of paces.

Gytha hesitated and then trotted after the sanctuary owner as if they'd known each other for years.

Gordon smiled nervously, but trusted she knew what she was doing. "Looks like I was wrong all along."

"May I present Gytha, the Surrey Puma," Simone said quietly. "She seems very well behaved."

Gordon tentatively reached out and stroked the enormous cat. It nuzzled against his leg and playfully wrapped its tail around his ankle. "She's beautiful," he said, casting an eye into the undergrowth and shivering. "I wonder if she's got a mate."

"I have a feeling we'll find out soon enough," Simone replied.

"How do you explain her colour?"

"She's what's known as melanistic," Simone replied. "The black pigmentation has been caused by a dominant gene. If you look closely you can still see her original markings through her fur."

Gordon noticed the slightly greyish tint closer to the cat's skin. "The papers are going to have a field day."

"Let's try to keep this quiet," she replied. "I think our new friend values her anonymity."

Gordon's face turned grim. "While you were busy, one of the policemen told me that there's a bird lying in the yard."

Simone stroked the puma's head and pressed her hand firmly into its lower back above the tail. The big cat sat obediently by the gate.

A fire crew had parked their engine in the middle of the yard and were dousing the flames licking the barn's remains. Thankfully none of the other outbuildings or the main house had been damaged. The barn next door had been bursting with battery chickens, which Gordon had already released into their large outdoor runs.

Simone guessed one of the birds must have been hit by the shotgun blast. "Where is he?"

Gordon led her to the eagle. The majestic bird was lying on his side in the mud. Ryker was standing next to him, a look of anguish on his face.

Simone knelt next to Seamus. Some shot had passed through his neck and chest. She felt for his heart but there was nothing. She shook her head and stood. "I'm afraid he's gone."

"If he and the falcon hadn't thrown themselves at Nigel," Gordon said quietly, "we might be lying there now."

Simone was fighting back the tears. "I know how we can honour him."

"I think that's a great idea," Gordon said, understanding what she meant and pulling her close. "Why don't we head home? The police can finish up here. And the birds can all stay in my warm stables."

She smiled and took his hand. "I hope you don't mind if Gytha comes too."

Despite the sadness of the situation, Gordon managed a brief laugh. "I can't wait to see the look on Avellana's face when she comes through the front door. That's one fight she won't be picking!"

19

The next morning Gordon woke early. He went downstairs in his dressing gown, put the kettle on and collected the paper from the doormat. He glanced through it and then took two cups of tea back to the bedroom. Ten minutes later he came down fully dressed and opened the curtains. He checked under the sofa in the living room to make sure Avellana wasn't cowering in terror, then unlocked the pantry and put his head round the door to check on Gytha. She was curled up in one of the dog baskets sound asleep, her purring deep and rhythmic. Gordon couldn't believe it when he noticed Lufu the fox and Avellana lying next to her, the puma's huge paw cradling them both.

"Now I've seen it all," he whispered, pulling the door closed behind him.

It was a beautiful morning outside, the chill of the night having been replaced by the summer warmth of the holiday weekend. Gordon crossed the yard to one of the stables. He'd laid out several hay bales and the birds had spent a comfortable night inside. "Good morning, my friends," he said. "I hope you're all feeling better today. When you're ready, we'll go and bury Seamus." He scattered a bag of grain into a pristine trough and left them to their breakfast.

"We need to keep our strength up," Ryker said. "Today is going to be another long day."

The birds felt rejuvenated by a good night's sleep and the food buoyed their mood further, but they were still sad to be burying their friend.

Gordon returned a few minutes later with a wooden

casket. It was heavy judging by the look on his face. He pulled the stable door wide open with his foot and the birds filed out. They followed him down the garden to the family plot. He'd already dug a hole, so he lowered the casket and began shovelling earth on top. He then said a short prayer thanking the eagle for saving him from the shotgun blast.

"I'll give you a moment alone," Gordon said eventually. He headed back to the yard to continue feeding his animals, which now included a hundred of Nigel's chickens.

Ryker gathered his friends round and drew Safiyya close. "Seamus gave his life so that Gordon could live," he said quietly. "And if it hadn't been for his kindness at the bird park, none of us would be here today. Many think that we birds live a life of freedom, that we are not bound by the laws of the earth, and that we can fly wherever we want without restriction. But for some of us life can be very different. Seamus was held against his will and mistreated by his human captors, yet last night he instinctively chose to help a human. He knew the difference between right and wrong, between good and bad, and he made the right decision for all of us. We owe him a debt of gratitude that none of us can possibly repay. So I ask that you keep him in your thoughts whenever life gets hard and you feel you can't go on. May his courage and strength guide us through our darkest times."

Cuthbert patted him on the back. "He would have appreciated that, mon ami. Thank you."

Ryker felt a surge of pride run through him and he bowed his head. "I know things haven't been easy for you either."

Cuthbert clasped his wings together and stood next to Seamus's grave. "Old friends pick up where they left off, no matter how much time has passed." He puffed out his chest. "And there's life in the old bugger yet. Let's celebrate that."

Algar gestured for quiet and turned to his son, his pride in his achievements obvious. "If it hadn't been for you, things might have turned out differently, Ryker. If we owe Seamus a debt, then we owe you one too. It was your strength that kept the flock together, your leadership guiding them through difficult times, your resolve that prepared them for the final battle. You've shown thoughtfulness and great courage and I'm very proud of you." He paused for a moment. "And I'm truly sorry for the way I've treated you over the years. Your mother forgave me my shortcomings, and I should have realised that you were not to blame for what happened to your sister."

Ryker let go of Safiyya and hugged his father. He knew his words were genuine. "That means a great deal to me, Dad. Thank you." He managed to fight back the tears this time and nodded towards their nests. He couldn't think of anything else to say other than, "I think we should go and get mum. She should be with us today."

Algar winked. "She's enjoying playing grandma now."

It was lunchtime when Gordon pulled out of the driveway in his tractor. He was towing a large trailer carrying Simone and the birds. Ryker finally felt able to relax. As they drew closer to Boxhill, they passed hundreds of people walking into the town. There would be a record turnout for the festival and race. The police had closed some of the roads so that only official vehicles could pass. A folk band played music on the pavement and all the shops had stands in the street. There was a real carnival atmosphere.

Gordon parked the tractor next to all the others. He climbed out of the cab and undid the tailgate so that Simone could join him. She was carrying a large rectangular

162

canvas, which she handed to an important-looking town official.

"Thanks, Simone," the man said. "Best of luck."

Gordon knew the birds would wait in the trailer so he and Simone wandered off to enjoy the food and drink at the vineyard stand.

Gordon had just finished a glass of the local white wine when he noticed a man shuffling papers and rehearsing his lines next to a rostrum on the opposite side of the road. "Simone," he said quietly, "I think the time has come to introduce ourselves to Mr Biggs."

"Promise me you won't lose your temper," she warned him.

He put his arm around her waist and smiled. "Worry not. I don't like scenes."

They walked over and Gordon held out his hand. "It's a pleasure to meet you, Craig," he said pleasantly.

Craig Biggs gripped his hand firmly, his ruddy face partially obscured by his bushy beard, his eyes flitting between them as if suspicious. "And you too, Mr...?" he let the question hang.

"Call me Gordon," the farmer said, gazing deep into the MP's beady little eyes. "You know who I am."

Biggs tightened his grip and fixed the farmer with a cold stare. "You're on my turf now, Gordon. Tread carefully." As if to emphasise his point, his moustache twitched angrily.

"That's where you're wrong, old boy," the farmer replied politely, his strong worker's hands easily matching the pressure exerted on them. "This is my home town and these are my friends. You should rethink giving your speech shortly. I don't think it'll be very well received."

Biggs tried to remove his hand but Gordon now held him in a painful grip. "You don't scare me. You're just a struggling farmer who is about to lose his business. Now let me go so I can get on with my official engagement."

Gordon noticed that the man's thick grey beard seemed to be developing a mind of its own. He increased his grip a little but smiled easily as if they were old friends chatting. "A letter arrived this morning from your former secretary."

"What do you mean?" Biggs asked, this clearly news to him. "She's not leaving."

"No, she isn't," Gordon replied, the satisfaction evident on his face. "You are. Your resignation will be accepted later on today, shortly after your arrest I should imagine."

"I've no idea what you're talking about," Biggs scoffed.

Gordon finally released him, noting with some satisfaction that the MP's hand was a bright and angry red. "Why don't you give me your speech and take a look at this instead?" He turned to Simone. "Would you do the honours?"

The sanctuary owner nodded. "With pleasure." She handed Biggs a file and walked back to the trailer.

Biggs massaged his hand and read the first few lines. "You'll never prove any of this, Gordon."

"I don't need to," Gordon replied casually, the deck stacked firmly in his favour. "We have a full confession from Nigel. You happen to be the chairman of the First Southern banking chain, and I know that you were trying to prop up the bank by acquiring a number of local farms on the cheap so you could sell them on for huge profits, thus destroying the livelihood of local farmers. But when you and Nigel discovered that falcons and other rare birds bred on my land, you saw the opportunity to make a fast buck. You bought the Feathered-Friends Park and began selling valuable eggs for new enclosures. You diversified into selling other birds for illegal cosmetic testing in the zoo's lab before hitting the jackpot." Gordon was in his element now and in full flow. "Through your list

164

of contacts you were introduced to the murky world of falconry. The birds are raced in the Middle East, with some competitions worth millions. You knew migratory birds nested on my land, so you and Nigel hatched a plan to trade in them. Suddenly it all made perfect sense. Anyway, I'm not telling you anything you don't already know so enjoy the rest of the festival, and keep an eye out for those irate Arabs."

Biggs took a deep breath before lashing out at Gordon but he'd barely moved before two burly policemen pounced. They'd been waiting behind the MP in case he tried to escape. They pinned his arms behind his back and read him his rights. There was a clink of metal as cuffs snapped shut on his wrists.

"I'll take this," Gordon said, picking up the MP's speech. "It had better be good." He nodded to the policemen and they carted Biggs off to a waiting car.

In the hustle and bustle of the festival no one gave the incident a second glance. Gordon walked over to the rostrum and spoke briefly with the mayor. The crowds in the meantime had filled the town centre to capacity and the stalls were doing a roaring trade in soft drinks and ice creams.

The town mayor spoke first. He apologised for MP Craig Biggs's absence but he'd been taken ill with food poisoning. He then introduced Gordon as their short-notice special guest instead.

The farmer stood on the rostrum and accepted the polite applause. He waited for quiet before launching into the speech, some of it adlibbed, the rest taken from the MP's notes. He praised the local farms and the vineyard for their produce and held up his glass of wine. As he brought the speech to a close he put the MP's notes aside and gripped both sides of the rostrum.

"As some of you may know, there was a fire on one of the farms east of here last night. I'm delighted to tell you that all of the animals survived, and the structural damage to the outbuildings can be repaired. I'm eternally grateful to Simone and the animal sanctuary for taking in the injured birds and nursing them back to health."

There was a huge roar of approval from the crowd, the applause lasting several minutes. Gordon almost looked embarrassed by the end but knew he had one more announcement to make. "I'd like to add that I received this letter from the ministry of agriculture and the land registry this morning." He held up the piece of paper for them all to see. "My initial request to have the land around the Redlands Forest and the chalk cliffs declared a nature reserve had been rejected, but I'm delighted to tell you that this decision has just been overturned." There was yet another cheer and Gordon was about to step down when the mayor joined him.

"I'd like to extend you our thanks for stepping in at such short notice," the mayor began. "Before you leave to watch the race from the wine tent, I'd like you to unveil the town's new coat of arms, which was voted for by the public from the contenders exhibited here today." He handed Gordon a large canvas covered with a red velvet cloth. "When you're ready."

The farmer pulled off the cover to another tremendous round of applause. He didn't know how she'd managed to paint such a magnificent piece in the few hours she'd had that morning, but he was delighted that Simone's entry had won. It showed a peregrine falcon standing next to the town's traditional cockerel while a huge golden eagle blended subtly into the background and stood guard over both.

He stepped off the podium and embraced her. "I can't believe you came up with something so beautiful. Congratulations."

She looked deep into his eyes. "I had wonderful models. Why don't we take them home for a well-earned rest?"

166

He led her through the crowd to the tractor. "No room for the puma?" he asked quietly.

She laughed. "Do you think they'd have believed us?"

"If someone did, they'd only have organised a hunting party," he replied. "We couldn't have that."

Gordon turned and waved to everyone and climbed into the trailer. "We'll have to wait for the race to come through first."

Simone checked her watch. "They're due any minute."

She'd hardly finished speaking when the cyclists rushed through the town centre in a blur. The crowd gave another enormous cheer and in no time at all the racers were climbing the twisting road onto Boxhill itself.

Gordon then climbed into the cab and started the tractor. It took a while to drive the three miles home as there were still hundreds of people arriving for the afternoon's festivities, but eventually Gordon parked the tractor in the barn and took Simone inside for a cup of tea and a slice of cake.

He brought the tray into the living room and set it down on a small wooden table by the fireplace. He was about to pour her a mug when the phone rang. He picked it up and listened for a few moments, then had his questions answered. After a couple of minutes, he hung up.

"That was my animal rights activist chum," he said. "Police have raided the lab and shut the park down while they conduct a full investigation into its dealings."

"What will happen to the birds?" she asked.

"Most will be released," he replied with a smile. "The rest will be shipped to zoos with impeccable reputations."

"Then this whole nasty episode is over," she said, her relief obvious.

"Thank goodness for that," he said. "Now we can turn our attention to each other."

She gripped his hand. "I'd like that."

*

Ryker hopped off the trailer and crossed the yard. He still couldn't believe the way events had unfolded and led him here. He had a new friend in Hawkins, a one-legged kestrel with a great sense of humour; then there was Naz, an owl all the way from the subcontinent, and a wise soul if ever there was one; they'd met Duke the crafty jackdaw up in London, and what an asset he'd turned out to be; Seamus the eagle would never be forgotten; but there was also Cuthbert and his brother Wilbur; Eadric the confused cockerel; and lastly Hatcher, the dippy pigeon. What a mix of personalities, Ryker thought; what unlikely allies!

He hugged Safiyya and watched the pigeon as he wandered aimlessly around the yard looking for food. "You know if it hadn't been for Hatcher, we'd never have gone to the airport and found Hawkins," he said after a while. "He and Asketil helped change the course of the final battle."

Hawkins, Duke and Naz hopped over to listen to what he had to say.

"And," Ryker continued, "we'd never have made it to London and met Duke either."

Hatcher cocked his head slightly but continued pecking for food.

"Nor would we have found our way to Feathered-Friends and rescued Seamus," Naz added.

"Makes you think, doesn't it?" Ryker said. He couldn't help but wonder if there was more to Hatcher than met the eye.

Duke nodded at the pigeon. "Surely you don't believe he could be acting that stupid."

Ryker shrugged. "If he was clever enough, he could."

Hatcher carried on pecking at the grain on the yard floor, apparently oblivious to the other birds.

After a moment they looked at each other and as one

shook their heads. "Nah!" they said, laughing and slapping each other on the back.

"No way," Duke said through the tears. "It's just not possible. Think of some of the things he said."

"What about the cuckoo chick in his nest?" Cuthbert asked. "That can't have been deliberate."

Naz shrugged. "He could have been feeding it disinformation."

Hawkins frowned. "What information?"

"Disinformation," Ryker said, chuckling.

Duke winked. "Oh, that information."

Cuthbert started laughing again and all the birds joined in.

Hatcher smiled to himself and suddenly appeared to notice that they were all having a jolly good time so he ambled over. "What's so funny?"

"Nothing really," Hawkins said. "We were just wondering about you."

Hatcher nodded knowingly. "I do that all the time."

"What do you think happened to the magpie?" Naz asked.

"Not once did she help the ravens or cuckoos in the battle," Ryker said. "I think she was a coward."

"Don't be ridiculous," Hatcher said, repeating his favourite line. He was about to explain himself when he appeared to lose his train of thought.

"See what I mean," Duke said.

"I want to thank you for all your help, Hatcher," Ryker said, the laughter lines creasing his face. "You're a good friend."

The pigeon puffed his chest out once more. "It was my pleasure."

Safiyya hugged him. "I'd like to thank you too."

Hatcher looked over his shoulder. "Me and who? The last I heard there was only one of me."

"Just you, Hatcher, just you," she said, letting him

wander back to his feed.

Ryker turned to his friends. "Will you excuse us for a moment?" He held out his wing and led Safi down to the bottom of the garden. He nodded towards the chalk cliffs. "Care to join me?"

They leaped into the air together and shared a few precious moments alone. Ryker suddenly rolled over and plucked an insect out of the sky. They flew across the field and landed on the ledge that they'd called home. Algar and Mercia stepped aside and showed them into the rebuilt nests.

"They're beautiful," Mercia said.

Ryker shared the insect between the chicks while Safi and his parents glowed with pride. "They'll grow up strong and healthy."

Algar put his wing around Mercia. "We have a small announcement to make. You've earned the right to live in Redlands. There's not enough food to support us all, so your mother and I will find a new home."

Ryker's face fell. "But, Dad!"

"Not another word, son," Algar said sternly, but with a twinkle in his eye. "We'll never be far away."

Mercia hugged them both. "And all your friends are here too."

They both leaped off the cliff and soared into the sunshine.

Ryker and Safi gazed across the fields with the afternoon breeze gently fanning their feathers. He looked at her and sensed she had something on her mind, something important. "What is it, darling?" he asked.

She drew him close and whispered in his ear, excitement in her voice. "Our family is about to get even bigger. I'm pregnant again."

THE END

Liam McCann can be contacted via
Twitter: @liambmccann
Facebook: The Battle of Boxhill
or on his website www.liambmccann.com